BEWARE!!
NOT READ THIS
BOOK FROM BEGINNING TO E

Me Tarzan. You

You're on holiday ly
for some real jungl quicksand,
swinging on vines!

Then you eat some enchanted fruit and start changing into a hideous scaly monster! Now tigers are the least of your worries.

You've got to find a way to get back to normal. And fast. Before your friends leave you behind in the jungle of doom!

But first, you'll have to escape a lake full of vicious piranhas. Or find your way out of an underground cavern. Or take your chances with a tribe of head-hunters!

You're in control of this scary adventure. You decide what will happen. And how terrifying the scares will be.

Start on PAGE 1. Then follow the instructions at the bottom of each page. You make the choices.

Make the right choices and live to tell the tale. Make the wrong choice . . . and BEWARE!

SO TAKE A LONG, DEEP BREATH, CROSS YOUR FINGERS AND TURN TO PAGE 1 NOW TO *GIVE YOURSELF GOOSEBUMPS!*

READER BEWARE—
YOU CHOOSE THE SCARE!

Look for more
GIVE YOURSELF GOOSEBUMPS adventures
from R.L. STINE:

Give Yourself Goosebumps

Deep in the Jungle of Doom

R.L. Stine

Hippo

Scholastic Children's Books
Commonwealth House, 1 – 19 New Oxford Street, London WC1A 1NU, UK
a division of Scholastic Ltd
London ~ New York ~ Toronto ~ Sydney ~ Auckland
Mexico City ~ New Delhi ~ Hong Kong

First published in the USA by Scholastic Inc., 1996
First published in the UK by Scholastic Ltd, 1999

Copyright © Parachute Press, Inc., 1996
GOOSEBUMPS is a trademark of Parachute Press, Inc.

ISBN 0 590 11403 4

Typeset by Rowland Phototypesetting Ltd, Bury St Edmunds, Suffolk
Printed by Cox & Wyman Ltd, Reading, Berks.

10 9 8 7 6 5 4 3 2 1

"All right, Junior Explorers, I direct your attention to this magnificent specimen of *Bromeliad aechmea . . .*"

On and on the guide, Mrs Wheedle, drones. You can't believe you're stuck on a nature study tour!

When you saw the brochure for the Junior Explorer Adventure Club at the front desk of your hotel, it looked great. Three days' hiking in the jungle with ten other kids your age and an "experienced jungle guide". How cool!

"Come on," you begged your parents. "We're in South America and you want me to sit by the pool all day? I could do that at home. Why did you take me to a foreign country if you didn't want to expose me to new things?"

Now you wish your parents had said NO! At least your best friend Zoe is with you on the hike. And, even though the guide is as boring as possible, the jungle *is* pretty cool. Heavy vines hang criss-crossed over the trail. Strange and beautiful flowers in deep colours sprout from every side.

As you follow Zoe, you notice a strange spiky flower with bright blue petals off to the side of the trail. Absent-mindedly, you reach out to touch it.

A sudden breeze makes the bright blue petals shiver.

"NOOOOOOOOO!" the flower screams!

You pull your hand back at the last second!

Race to PAGE 2.

"NOOOOOOOOO!" the scream continues. "Don't touch that flower!"

It's only Mrs Wheedle.

"What's wrong?" you ask. "Is it poisonous? Does it shoot venom or something cool?"

"Of course not!" Mrs Wheedle huffs. "That flower is an endangered species. You could have killed it!"

She turns and marches back to the front of the group.

"Whew! That was a close one!" Zoe says, brushing her fringe away from her eyes. "For a second there, I thought something exciting was actually going to happen!"

Zoe's cool. Very cool. That's one of the reasons she's your best friend. She has a sarcastic remark for every situation. And she's not scared of anything.

That's why you know she's just as anxious as you are to break away from the group and do some *real* exploring.

Just a moment ago, through the trees, you saw something else that was definitely worth checking out.

There it is again. Off to the right. About twenty metres away. Incredible! Your heart skips a beat at what you see.

Find out what it is on PAGE 37!

"THREE!"

The king claps his hands three times and the servants turn the timepiece over. You do the same thing to the miniature timepiece in your hand. The sand pours through the glass. You tuck the baby hourglass into your shirt pocket. It fits perfectly.

"You have one Palooka! NOW BRING ME THREE PIECES OF GOLD!" the king bellows.

You glance round the chamber. There are tunnels everywhere.

"Come on!" you shout at Zoe. "Let's go!"

The two of you head for the biggest tunnel leading away from the chamber.

You have one Palooka to find the gold.

Just how long is a Palooka anyway? you wonder.

Turn to PAGE 58 to start the quest.

No way are you going to throw away millions of dollars' worth of jewels!

You scrunch up as best you can and watch as the pointed rock formations inch closer and closer to you.

Ouch! An emerald scrapes your shoulder.

You huddle between the rocks, holding your breath.

A giant diamond is coming straight for your head!

One centimetre more and you're history. You squeeze your eyes shut tight.

With a screech, the walls stop closing in.

Wow! Just in time not to crunch your head!

You open your eyes. You try to move but you can't. You're pinned in place by a fortune in jewels.

You wait and wait, but the walls don't open up again.

In fact, they NEVER open up again. You're trapped there.

For ever.

But look on the bright side. You always wanted to die a millionaire.

THE END

"Excuse me," you call to Unger. "I don't mean to slow us down, but I'm dying of hunger. Do you have anything I could snack on?"

"Of course," says Unger. "We never go anywhere without plenty of food." She opens the tiger-skin sack slung over her shoulder. Unger takes out a handful of flowers and passes them round. The flowers are edible! They're delicious. You're glad you asked!

After a few more minutes of marching through the humid green jungle, Unger brings the group to a halt. You're standing in front of a cave. It's dark and lined with jagged rocks. A warm, dry breeze wafts out from the cave's mouth.

"That's where the Fireheart tree is," Unger tells you and Ben. She points to the small cave. "Follow the tunnel until you reach a big cave. In the centre will be the tree."

"Thank you so much!" you tell the Warrior Women.

"It is our pleasure to defeat the spells of the Muglani," Unger replies. "Good luck, my little friends!"

She pats you and Ben on the back and turns to leave.

"Oh, one last thing about the cave," Unger remarks. "Beware of the guard dragon!"

Turn to PAGE 87.

"GRRRRRRRRR!" The gargoyle growls at you from the shore and slashes one of its razor-sharp claws through the air.

Meanwhile, you're starting to lose feeling above your knees now. You never knew water could be this cold. Things are looking grim.

"Let's be calm about this," you say. "There must be something we can do."

"Yeah, right," Zoe moans, rolling her eyes. "Why don't we just swim right up the waterfall!"

"Ha-ha, very funny!" you retort. Sometimes Zoe's sarcasm isn't so cool.

But you stare at the waterfall anyway. The water pounds down from the jagged cliffs above. Sunlight turns the falling streams of water many deep shades of blue and green. But that's not what you're looking at. There's something else. You think you can make out the outline of something *behind* the falls.

Something big. Something dark. Is it another stone beast?

Hurry to PAGE 31 and find out!

You stand in the clearing, waiting for the person who is coming closer. The sound of leaves rustling grows louder. You cross your legs and smile, trying not to look scary. You hope that whoever it is will help you!

Ben, one of the kids from the Junior Explorer Adventure Club, bursts into the clearing. It looks as if he's reading some kind of a comic book or a pamphlet. He keeps glancing down at his book then back up. As if he's looking at a map.

At first Ben doesn't even notice you. You remember talking with Zoe about him. He's a real bookworm and kind of a geek. His red hair is tousled and his glasses are slightly crooked. Freckles cover his whole face.

Ben sees the table and rushes over to it in excitement. You clear your throat a bit to let him know you're there.

Ben spins round from the table. His eyes grow big as he stares at you. He stares at your clothes. Your trainers. Your terrifying face. Your gruesome claws.

Dropping the pamphlet, Ben points at you.

"You're . . . you're . . . I know who you are!" he stutters. "And I know how you got that way!"

Catch up with Ben on PAGE 21.

8

You are tramping through the jungle, following your classmates. Zoe is right behind you. You've been doing nothing but studying plants all morning! This is the most boring holiday ever!

Oh, no! Not only have you been zapped out of the cave, but you've also been zapped back in time!

You're back where you started . . . and everything you learned inside the mountain is starting to fade in your memory. It's as if the whole adventure never happened.

Pretty soon Mrs Wheedle will lead the class off in search of that funny flower. And you and Zoe will sneak away!

Try to remember this: when the stone gargoyle chases you, HEAD FOR THE CLEARING THIS TIME!

Now go back to PAGE 1. Good luck!

Zoe's right. What do you owe that nasty cave king, anyway? He tried to make you slaves!

"Forget I even brought it up," you mumble. You slip the timepiece back into your pocket and keep climbing.

A metre or so up the stone ladder and you and Zoe reach the surface. How sweet the fresh air smells! You hope you never see another cave in your life!

Together, you and Zoe find your way back to the Junior Explorers. They're not too hard to find. They make so much noise, talking and shouting.

Mrs Wheedle is upset because no one's found the rare flower, but it seems like the other kids had fun!

You keep the timepiece hidden during the rest of the day. Until after dinner, when you inspect it by the light of your lantern.

Should I keep it or sell it? you ask yourself. You hold the pretty hourglass up to the soft lantern light.

That's when you hear the sound of hands fumbling to open the flaps to your tent.

"Zoe?" you call. "Is that you?"

"No!" comes a gruff whisper. You recognize the voice!

It's the king of the cave people!

Race to PAGE 121.

10

A puff of mist rises from the pool of lava. Through the mist appears a fierce, sinister shape—a dragon. Short spikes cover its head and run down its spine. Though it's not gigantic, it looks quite deadly.

The dragon has rows of jagged teeth and sharp rippling scales. Two evil-looking green eyes with a stripe of fiery red down the middle peer hatefully at you and Ben.

"I don't think we can fight it!" Ben yells. He scrambles to pick up his club.

"But we've got to!" you shout. You tighten your grip on your stick. Your body is trembling from head to webbed foot.

HISS! The dragon slithers right through the lava moat. As it creeps towards you, you hear its sharp claws scratch at the rock.

"Let's go!" Ben begs. "Let's run! Now!"

If you run, go to PAGE 13.
If you try to defeat the dragon, go to PAGE 36.

The stone beast is right behind you!

"This way, Zoe," you call as you race down the path that leads to the clearing. You know you can scare the gargoyle with the heavy sticks and stones you see on the ground.

ROAR! The beast's voice explodes through the jungle. Birds send out warning calls to each other. Your heart races even faster than your feet.

You stumble into the clearing. The ground is covered in fine, green grass. The sticks on the grass are just the size of baseball bats.

"Quick," Zoe shouts to you. "Grab a stick." She has already armed herself with a heavy club from the ground.

Out of the corner of your eye, you see a high table off to the side. Some weird little balls are hanging off the tabletop. But you don't have time to check them out.

Instead, you reach down and pick out a stick and a nice, softball-sized stone. You spin round to face the beast.

Growling deeply, the gargoyle bares its teeth. It rips through the air with five razor-sharp claws.

Then it pounces into the clearing!

Turn to PAGE 48 and get ready to rumble!

12

"Let's take the tunnel that looks wet," you say to Zoe. "There might be some sort of a stream, and sometimes gold washes up in a stream."

"Good thinking," Zoe agrees. "I'll go first."

She steps cautiously into the slippery tunnel.

BAM! She wipes out and starts sliding down the tunnel.

"Careful," she calls back to you as she skids down the chute. "It's slipperyyyyy!"

You have no choice but to follow her! So you take a flying leap and jump head first down the tunnel, as if it were a water slide.

ZOOM to PAGE 118.

The dragon draws nearer. Spiky white teeth snap at you. It eyes you viciously with its fiery pupils.

"You're right!" you cry. "We can't fight that thing! Let's get out of here!"

You and Ben drop your clubs and race towards the exit. You stumble over the rough rocks.

Because your backs are turned, you don't see the dragon dip its mouth into the lava pool and slurp up a mouthful of molten rock. With a huge puff, the dragon spits fire at you.

The flames bellow down the tunnel after you, catching up with you in no time at all.

You told everyone in Mrs Wheedle's group you were a big-time explorer who could survive any adventure!

Looks like you were wrong.

Liar, liar, pants on fire!

THE END

"Let's take the tunnel that goes down!" you say. You pull the timepiece out of your pocket to check it. "Hurry, we've only got about two-thirds of a Palooka left!"

"Even if we do get the gold in time, do you think we'll make it back to the group before they take off?" Liz asks, glancing at her clunky watch. "It's already two-thirty! We only have half an hour left!"

"Let's worry abut the gold first. If we get out of this mess, we'll meet up with Mrs Wheedle somehow!" you remark.

You follow Zoe down the narrow tunnel. This one is not as well-lit as the other. There is only one lantern about every six metres. Even though Zoe is right in front of you, sometimes you bump into her because you can't see her.

"Ouch!" Zoe complains. "Walk further behind me. You don't have to walk on my heels."

"Sorry!" you answer. "I'll hang back a little."

The tunnel twists and turns. Zoe gets so far ahead of you that you feel as if you're alone.

Your trainers crunch on the loose rocks on the floor of the path. The sound echoes down the passageway.

You can hear your heart beating. BUM-bum. BUM-bum.

Flip to PAGE 33.

"Hmmmmmm," Cronby says, leaning up against the boulder. "Let me think . . ."

"Don't think for too long," you tell him, pulling the hourglass out of your pocket. "I've only got a third of a Palooka left!"

"Okay, if you're so brave," the troll says, "then you must read lots of scary books. Have you ever heard of R.L. Stine?"

"Of course!" you shout. Your voice echoes down the hallway. You're a GOOSEBUMPS expert! You're going to ace this question!

"In the book, *Revenge of the Garden Gnomes*, a vicious animal scares the garden gnomes away. Is it a bat? Or a dog?"

Easy, you think to yourself.

Either say: "It was a bat!" and flip to PAGE 90.

Or say: "It was a dog!" and flip to PAGE 30.

You make a hard left and dive off the path. Out of sight of the hunters, you quickly slip into the giant flower.

Immediately the pink and white petals close in around you. You couldn't have asked for a better hiding-place. You're completely hidden from view.

The sweet smell inside the flower almost over-powers you. It makes you want to sneeze. So you hold your breath.

"Where did it go?" James calls.

"This way," Gwen cries, leading the hunting party right past your hiding-place.

Whew! It worked! The hunters pass you by.

You catch your breath and push at the flower petals with your hands and feet.

It won't open up!

You push harder. You strain with all your might. You scratch at the petals with your strong monster claws.

But nothing works. You're trapped inside!

The petals tighten round you and slowly begin chewing.

That's right, chewing. Not all flowers just drink water, you know.

First you were a kid, then you were a monster. Now you're just plant food.

THE END

You can't believe your eyes! The bat is the most hideous thing you've ever seen. Its wings are folded round its hairy brown body. It has enormous ears that are so thin you can see the veins running through them. Two beady black eyes are watching you and Cronby carefully.

The bat opens its mouth and talks! "What did you say about me?"

"Oh, no!" Cronby shouts. "I wasn't talking to you!"

"I heard you," the bat says. "You said 'naughty bat'!"

"I wasn't talking to you, I swear!" Cronby stammers.

"I'll teach you to call people names!" the bat squeaks.

"I think I'll just be going," you mutter, trying to slip away.

"Oh, no you don't," the bat squeaks, turning to you. "I heard you call me a 'bad bat'."

You try to argue with the bat, telling it that you just said "big bat".

But bats seem to think they have very good hearing!

So much for that theory! But one thing this bat does have is very good teeth. Too bad for you and Cronby.

THE END

"I don't want to scare them!" you tell Ben quietly. "I'll just explain who I am. They'll understand everything after I eat the Fireheart fruit and turn back into myself."

"Who's there?" barks Mrs Wheedle. "Is that one of my Explorers? Step out where I can see you!"

"It's just me," you call. "Don't be scared! I can explain!" You step out from behind the bush.

Mrs Wheedle takes one look at your sharp teeth, fishy grey skin, and huge bulging eyes and faints. THUMP!

And just like that, the whole rest of the group passes out, too. THUMP! THUMP! THUMP! THUMP, THUMP! THUMP, THUMP!

You and Ben can't help but laugh. "I tried not to scare them!" you say. Stepping over Mrs Wheedle, you pluck one of the ripe, red Fireheart fruits. You sink your teeth into it.

Immediately you feel your skin tighten and your head start to shrink. It happens so quickly that you don't bother finishing the fruit. You're a kid again! More or less . . .

Back at the hotel, you tell the whole story during dinner with your family. They all think you're joking until a fly lands on the tablecloth. Zap! Your long, sticky tongue shoots out and catches the fly.

Looks like you should have eaten the whole Fireheart fruit. But then, there's a little monster inside everyone, in

THE END.

"Get BACK!" you shout, turning to face the cave creatures.

"Yeah!" yells Zoe. "Get LOST!"

You pick up a stone and hurl it at the creatures. It hits one of them right on the head.

"WAAAHHH!" it wails.

Zoe throws a rock.

The cave creatures turn round and run like crazy!

They're bawling like babies!

"Yes!" you exclaim.

"We did it!" Zoe shouts. You turn to her and give her a high five.

"Now let's get out of here before we melt!" you say.

"Right!" Zoe agrees. "I'm so sweaty, you could pour me into a bucket."

Race to PAGE 86.

20

As fast as you can, you empty your pockets of the jewels. You're just small enough to slip out into the tunnel before the ceiling meets the floor with a resounding crunch.

A spray of crunched jewels showers your back as you race down the tunnel to meet Zoe.

You carefully slide the timepiece out of your shirt pocket. The Palooka is nearly up—there's only about a centimetre of sand in the glass! Not a second to lose.

"Zoe! Are you there?" you call out.

"I've found the last piece of gold!" she answers. "But I don't know how to get it out!"

Zoe leads you down a tunnel to a small cave. A glassy pool of water is in the centre of the cave. And right in the centre of the pool, you see it.

"I can't believe it!" you exclaim.

What do you see? Look closer on PAGE 100.

"You're one of the kids from my Junior Explorers Club, aren't you?" Ben asks as he steps over to you. "You must have sneaked away from the group just like I did."

You're so glad he's not scared of you!

"Yes," you manage to say. The goo in your throat is sliding away. Or maybe you're just learning how to speak through it.

"And I bet that you came into this clearing, saw this table, and ate one of the magic fruits from this basket!

"It turned you into a fish monster! You fell right into their trap!" he declares.

Suddenly, Ben lifts his nose and sniffs the air. A dopey smile spreads over his face.

As if in a trance, he stumbles to the table and grabs a banana from the basket. He holds it close to his nose and inhales the delicious odour. You know just what he's feeling!

"No! Ben!" you shout. "Don't eat the fruit!" Your voice still comes out all froggy.

Ben peels the banana!

If he eats it he'll probably turn into a monster, too!

Try to stop him on PAGE 79.

You get down on your hands and knees in front of the small dirt tunnel.

"Good luck," Zoe says. "I hope you find the way out!"

"See you in five minutes. Here goes nothing!" you say as you start tunnelling through the hole.

You crawl on your belly through the dark passageway. Rich earth from the sides of the tunnel covers your whole body. It's caked all over your face and jammed under your fingernails. Finally, you squeeze out of the tunnel with a plop! You're outside in the jungle!

The only problem is: you're in some kind of a pit! Steep, square walls go up about five metres.

It's great to be out of the cave and all those dark, winding tunnels, but am I really better off now than I was before? you wonder while staring at the smooth walls of the pit.

You've got a tough decision to make: should you go back for Zoe now? Your five minutes are almost up. Or should you try to get out of the pit first to make sure that you *can* get out?

Turn to PAGE 113 to go back for Zoe first.
Turn to PAGE 80 to try getting out of the pit.

Where did Zoe go, anyway? Wasn't she right behind you? Or was she too chicken?

You turn to scramble back to the mouth of the cave. But you stop to listen when you hear a voice.

"There's your supper," someone says. It's Zoe's voice! It's echoing through the cave. "Now you'll let me go, right?"

Supper? Let me go? Who's she talking to? What's going on?

That's when the sides of the cave turn smooth. And the floor starts to move, like a long, pink escalator.

Like a long, pink tongue.

With a horrified gasp, you realize why the air in this cave feels so humid ... You're not in a cave, you're in the mouth of a giant stone beast, as big as a whole mountain!

How is that possible? How did Zoe know? And why would your best friend betray you?

Those are good questions, but unfortunately you don't have time to worry about them.

In fact, you only have about five seconds before you land in the beast's acid-filled stomach. Four ... three ... two ... one ...

THE END

You carefully make your way towards the area you were exploring earlier with the Junior Explorers.

That tree with the fruits that look just like little hearts must be around here somewhere, you think to yourself.

You push away some thick vines and see before you a small clearing in the jungle. Right in the centre is the tree you saw earlier. You really hope it's the Fireheart tree!

It is a small tree with dull, flat leaves and grey bark. The branches are loaded down with pretty red heart-shaped fruits.

"Look!" you exclaim. "Ben, I've found the tree I was telling you about!"

"Shhhh!" Ben grabs you by the arm and pulls you back behind a fuzzy, flowering bush.

"Quiet," he whispers. "Someone's coming!"

Hurry to PAGE 57.

You're trapped in a pit with two tiger skeletons!

They circle you slowly. The wind whistles through their bones. Their jaws snap open and closed. You can tell they're dying to take a bite out of you.

They don't have stomachs, so you reckon they can't really eat you. But they still have all their teeth!

You back into the corner, being careful not to step on any more bones.

The tigers approach, their tails clicking softly as they lash from side to side.

You remember an old jungle film you once saw. The hero sang to a wild tiger and put it to sleep. Maybe that would work on a tiger skeleton, too!

Or maybe you could leap up on one of the tigers' heads and make a jump for the edge of the pit. You're pretty athletic.

Either way, you've got to act quickly!

To sing a song for the tigers and try to calm them, turn to PAGE 117.

To make a jump for it, turn to PAGE 59.

You can't see round the boulder to see who's wearing the weird little shoe, but you're sure that whoever it is had something to do with the disappearance of your friend.

"Who's there?" you repeat.

"Just me—your friendly neighbourhood troll!" A tiny man steps out from behind the rock. He carries a bright lantern that casts a flood of light in the tiny chamber.

The troll is wearing a cute little mountain climber's outfit—complete with lederhosen and striped white-and-green stockings. A white beard covers his wrinkled face. He would look like a tiny clown, but he has an evil expression on his face. His mouth is set in a hard line and his eyes, you realize with shock, are RED.

"Where's my friend?" you ask the troll.

"Well, that's no way to greet someone!" the fellow snaps. He walks over to you. He comes up to your waist. "My name is Cronby. What's yours?" He extends his hand up to you. He leans towards you with his hand out, scowling. There's something wicked in those red eyes . . .

Do you shake his hand? Go to PAGE 29.

Or do you avoid his handshake? Turn to PAGE 81.

You pull the gummy leaf off your face. Your leg is stuck fast in some kind of hole. Blinking to clear your eyes, you gaze down at your foot.

That's when you see that the hole you've just stepped in is no ordinary hole.

It's a giant anthill of enormous red ants.

"Pull your leg out before the ants get angry!" Ben advises. "And hurry up! We've got to find the Fireheart tree!"

"I can't pull my foot out! It's stuck!" you exclaim. You pull with all your might. Bending down, you scrape at the anthill with your sharp new claws. You huff and wheeze with the effort. It's no good!

The red ants begin to swarm round your ankle!

"Quick, Ben!" you shout. "Grab that stick and try to dig my leg out!" You nod your head towards a big stick on the ground.

"I don't know if that will work," Ben says. "Maybe I should pour some water from my canteen on to the ants. That would drown them! What do you want me to do?"

To have Ben dig your leg out with the stick, go to PAGE 60.

To have him drown the ants, go to PAGE 89.

The Warrior Woman's spear is aimed right at your heart!

You feel the sharp stone point of her spear graze your arm as the spear comes closer. You squeeze your eyes shut.

At the last possible moment, the head Warrior Woman flicks the blade to the left. Instead of plunging the spear into you, she cuts one of the ropes of the net.

You and Ben tumble down to the ground!

"Hee-hee-hee!" The Warrior Women guffaw as if it's the funniest thing they've ever seen.

"I'm glad they think it's funny," Ben mumbles. He polishes his glasses on his shirt. You are both lying on the ground, covered in dirt. The head Warrior Woman holds up her hand for silence. The other women stop laughing abruptly.

The Warrior Woman drops to all fours right next to you. She peers into your face, examining you closely. You can see your own reflection in her large, black pupils. Your gooey grey skin, your big glassy black eyes, your rows of sharp teeth.

The Warrior Woman reaches up to scratch her back. A tiger-skin bag hanging from her side falls open. Inside you see a shrunken head!

You draw back in shock.

Go to PAGE 95.

You don't want to be rude so you lean down to shake his hand. As you're shaking his hand, the troll gazes into your eyes and smiles a slow, menacing smile.

Why, those eyes aren't so bad after all! you think to yourself. I can see my reflection in them! And there's something else.

You gaze deeper into the troll's twirling red eyes.

There's your mum! And your dad! There's your house! *What are they doing in there?*

The eyes twist you around. You feel dizzy. The rocks of the cave are spinning. Yet you search deeper into his eyes.

Your mum and dad are crying! They're crying over someone . . .

You look deeper. Deeper. Deeper into the red eyes.

THEY'RE CRYING OVER YOU! Because they'll never see you again.

While you've been gazing deeper and deeper into the tiny man's eyes, he's been hypnotizing you. He has made you his slave for the rest of your life.

Too bad you couldn't resist that handshake, 'cause now you'll never be able to resist *anything* the troll tells you to do.

THE END

"It was a dog. Joe and Mindy's dog, Buster," you say with confidence.

You watch as the troll's face turns scarlet. His skin almost matches the fiery colour of his eyes.

"NO! NO! NO!" he screams.

"You mean I've got it wrong?" you gasp.

"No! You've got it right! I made the question too easy!"

Excellent! You did it!

"NO! NO! NO!" Cronby screeches, throwing his body on the ground and hammering it with his tiny fists. "I haven't had a meal in twenty years," the troll moans.

"That's *your* problem! I won fair and square!" you declare. "Now show me where Zoe is and give me my gold!"

"Why don't you give me one last chance? We could bet for another piece of gold . . ." he wheedles. "That way you would have all three and you could go free."

You hesitate. "I don't know."

"Come on, it'll be fun!" he pleads. "I'll ask you another R.L. Stine question. After all, time *is* running out."

It's a hard call, but you've got to make a decision.

Do you bet for the third piece of gold? Turn to
PAGE 114.

Or do you grab Zoe and the two pieces of gold
and get away from the troll? Turn to PAGE 38.

No. It's not another stone beast you see behind the waterfall. It's the mouth of a cave!

"We might not be able to go *up* the waterfall," you say to Zoe. "But maybe we can go *through* it! Come here and look!" Clutching your floating stick, you paddle over towards the pounding falls and mist. Zoe follows you.

"Cool!" Zoe shouts. "There's a cave behind the falls! Maybe we can crawl through and find a way out of this mess!"

You take a deep breath and dive down—stick and all—under the tremendous spray created by the waterfall. The water pushes you down. For a moment, your eyes and ears fill with the pounding foam.

When you come up again, you are behind the sheet of water in the mouth of the cave. The sunlight shines through the mist, creating tiny rainbows in the air. It's pretty to look at the pool through the waterfall. The cave behind you isn't nearly so pretty.

Dark jagged rocks cut out from its black mouth. A warm, moist wind blows against your face.

Then you feel something slimy brush against your leg underwater. What was that? you think. But before you can think again, IT GRABS YOUR FOOT AND PULLS YOU UNDER!

Quick! Splash over to PAGE 125.

"It's 'Tanya the Terror'!" you declare with pride.

"WRONG! WRONG! WRONG!" Cronby shouts with glee. "I win! I win!"

Oh, no! You've got the answer wrong!

You get a sinking feeling in the pit of your stomach.

So does Cronby, soon enough. Except that in *his* stomach, what's sinking is you and Zoe!

THE END

You stumble along the darkly-lit tunnel, listening to your heartbeat.

How will you find three pieces of gold when it's so dark you can hardly see your hand in front of your face?

BUM-bum. BUM-bum. BUM-bum. Your heartbeat makes the only sound.

I can't even hear Zoe's footsteps any more, you think to yourself as you tramp through the passageway.

That's when the tunnel *ends*. That's right. You walk smack into a rounded stone wall.

You're in a small cave. Huge boulders block the path forward. It's a dead end.

Where did Zoe go? She was right in front of you . . .

Your heartbeat speeds up! BUM-BUM. BUM-BUM. BUM-BUM.

Where is she?

Look for her on PAGE 104.

"Let's go back to that big tunnel and choose another direction!" Zoe shouts as you race back the way you came.

"Okay," you pant. Sweat trickles down the back of your neck. "We just need to find one more piece of gold!" you exclaim, pulling the timepiece from your pocket and examining it. "We've got about a quarter of a Palooka left!"

"By the way," Zoe says, "thanks for saving me from the troll!"

"No problem!" you answer.

Finally you reach the big branch of the tunnel. It's nice to be able to see well again—the lanterns that line the walls of the main tunnel flicker brightly.

You glance down the tunnel in both directions. To the right you see a tunnel that leads to a lot of little passageways. There are a lot of options that way, but it might be easy to get lost.

To the left is one big tunnel that looks wet. If there's an underground stream it would be the perfect place to search for gold, but it might be slippery.

Either head for the group of tunnels on PAGE 109.

Or brave the slippery tunnel on PAGE 12.

Gasp! You can't breathe on dry land any more! It makes no sense! You were just walking around and breathing a few minutes ago. It's as if your transformation into a fish monster is finally complete!

Dizziness overtakes you. You collapse on the ground. Suddenly it occurs to you: you've got to make it back into the water, where you can breathe through your gills.

Inch by inch, you pull yourself back to the river's edge. Plop! You throw yourself into the racing water.

What a joy it is to have the cold, clear water streaming through your gills!

I suppose I won't be getting any help from Mrs Wheedle, you sigh to yourself as you paddle down the river. Unless she comes in for a dip!

It turns out to be a pretty good life, living in the river. There are plenty of small fish to eat, and sometimes you even hunt alligators.

Whenever humans come swimming, you try to explain to them who you are. But as soon as you get their attention, they never stick around long enough to find out.

They may not know who you used to be. But they know who you are now. You're a legend. Famous throughout the world. They call you . . . the Abominable Fish Monster!

THE END

36

"I've got to fight the dragon! I can't leave without getting one of those fruits!" you exclaim. "If I don't get one, I'll be stuck looking like a monster for the rest of my life!"

"Okay," Ben agrees courageously. "We'll fight the dragon!"

Just then you remember something you learned in school about lizards. Maybe it will work on a dragon!

"Don't move, Ben!" you command. "Some lizards can only see movement. Maybe it won't be able to see us if we hold still."

You're right. After you and Ben stop moving, the dragon seems confused. It sniffs at the air and scans the cave with its green-and-red eyes, but it doesn't see you. The dragon loses interest and crawls back behind the tree.

"I'm going to grab a fruit, very slowly," you whisper.

You tiptoe up to the lava pool, moving at the pace of a slow-motion replay. You slowly reach over the small lake of boiling, steaming molten rock.

Turn to PAGE 82.

About twenty metres off to the right, through the criss-crossing branches and leaves of the jungle, you see a bush.

A big bush of vines . . . with feet!

That's right, two clawed feet carved in stone are sticking out from under the clinging vines.

You figure it could be one of those tribal ruins in the jungle you've read about.

You've heard there used to be some pretty dangerous tribes of head-hunters in the area! You're dying to find out if they still exist.

Head-hunters shrink people's heads! And they make sacrifices to ancient statues carved in stone. At least that's what you've heard. Mrs Wheedle would have everyone thinking the most dangerous thing in the jungle was a bee. Or maybe an aphid—they eat endangered plants!

"Zoe," you call up to her. "Look over there! There's something weird about that bush. I wish we could go and check it out!"

"I've got an idea!" Zoe says with a gleam in her eye.

You've been friends with Zoe for almost your whole life. And you know that when you see that gleam in her eye, it means you're about to get into trouble—usually a fun kind of trouble—but always big trouble!

Find out what kind of trouble on PAGE 64.

"I'm not going to risk Zoe's life on a bet," you answer. "Now hand over my gold."

The troll hands you the gold nuggets with tears in his eyes. He swivels round and pushes a piece of moss on the huge boulder behind him. The stone rolls to the side to reveal a closet. Zoe is sitting there on the ground with her arms crossed over her chest.

"He pushed me in here and locked me in!" she yells.

"Quick!" you say to her as you help her up. "I won two pieces of gold, but we're running out of time!"

Zoe gets to her feet. Cronby kicks at the dust on the tunnel floor, looking disappointed.

"Wait just one second," Zoe says, lifting the troll up by his collar. "I have to finish up something with this little guy." Zoe pushes Cronby into the closet and presses the moss button.

"That's what you get for trapping people!" she shouts as the stone rolls into place.

"Come on!" you shout.

Together you race back through the tunnel.

You only need one more piece of gold! But where are you going to find it?

Start by looking on PAGE 34.

The Warrior Women are closing in on you with their spears. And they want to make Hackey Sacks out of your heads!

Time to SCRAM! you think. And without a word, you pick Ben up and take off.

You slip past the Warrior Women and race through the jungle. The exotic flowers and plants blur before your eyes as you run.

The Warrior Women hoot and holler behind you. Even though they are old, they run fast! And carrying Ben is weighing you down. They are right on your trail. Arrows zing past you and stab into the trees.

"Oh, NO!" Ben cries. You skid to a stop.

Ahead of you the ground falls off into a dark pit filled with bubbling, oozing tar.

An arrow flies over your shoulder and lands in the tar. The tar swallows it with a little burp that pops with a splat of gooey tar.

A vine dangles right in front of you.

"What do we do?" Ben asks.

To swing on the vine, go to PAGE 54.
To jump over the pit, go to PAGE 75.

40

"Let's try the door," you shout to Zoe. You grab the handle to the blue door and twist it with all your strength. It pops open and you and Zoe slip inside.

You slam the door behind you.

BANG! The creatures strike at the door in anger. BANG!

You're in a very dark room. It's not very big either. You can see dimly by the torchlight flooding under the door.

"Where are we?" you ask Zoe.

"I don't know, but at least we're away from those sponge-headed freaks," she answers.

BANG! The creatures pound on the door. They want in.

"I can't believe we got away from them," you add. "I thought we were definitely history!"

"Don't worry," Zoe remarks, "we may *still* be history!"

"Ha-ha, very funny," you answer. How can she be sarcastic at a time like this?

BANG! BANG! The cave creatures slam on the door.

"This place gives me the creeps!" Zoe declares.

"Me, too," you say. You feel chilled to the bone. You turn your head and see a flash of movement.

"Who's there?" you ask nervously. Good question . . .

The answer lies on PAGE 92.

You squirm and struggle, trying to break free from the Warrior Women. Three of them are holding on to you! Three other Warrior Women have got Ben. You can't move!

The women are incredibly strong. They bind your hands and feet with cord that looks as if it's been made out of plant stalks. The ancient Warrior Women lift you into the air and carry you through the jungle.

"Ben, what do we do now?" you ask him as you bounce along on the shoulders of the Warrior Women. "Did your booklet give you any ways to fight the Muglani?"

"No," Ben mumbles. "If only we had tried to jump over the tar pit! Maybe then we would have got away!"

"Maybe," you answer. "Or maybe if we had accepted their help in the first place!"

You two will have plenty of time to discuss it.

Soon, your shrunken heads will be hanging side by side on the magic table in the clearing. One little fish head. And another little one with glasses.

You two can HANG OUT together all you want!

THE END

42

You and Zoe dash off the path into the jungle. You hear Mrs Wheedle yelling behind you. "QUUUUUIIIIIIET!" You can picture her, red-faced and out of breath.

All the noise settles down and Mrs Wheedle starts talking again. You stay very still and listen from your hiding-place behind a big tree.

"We've got two good hours of hiking left to get to our camp-site for tonight. That gives us until three o'clock to find that *kerritatlocus*! Now everyone, *follow me!*"

It worked. They're looking for that flower. And as long as you hook back up with them again before three o'clock, they may never know you've been gone.

"Zoe, did you really see the kerritatloca-whatever?"

"No way!" she says, grinning from ear to ear. "But now we get to explore!"

You make your way through the dense leaves and vines towards the stone feet that caught your eye before.

"Here it is, Zoe!" you shout. "There must be a statue underneath these vines."

You both get a good grip on the creeping vines and yank them back. Your blood runs cold at what you see . . .

Rush to PAGE 47.

"Let's go back to where we were earlier," you say to Ben as you leave the clearing. "After all, that's where I thought I saw the Fireheart fruit."

"Cool!" Ben bounds ahead of you, pushing the heavy foliage out of his way as you both climb up a steep slope.

"Now I see why they use those big knives in the movies," he declares over his shoulder. "These leaves are really thick!"

A soft rain begins to fall. The water feels good on your gooey skin. You and Ben are making your way back to Mrs Wheedle's meeting spot when you come to a big gnarled tree.

You hear a rustling at your feet.

Suddenly you are snatched up into the air, along with Ben.

You've been caught in a huge net!

Drag yourself to PAGE 44.

You are hanging suspended from the giant tree in a big net. Tight, tough ropes criss-cross every which way.

"Who put this net here?" you ask Ben worriedly. "Do you think it was the medicine men?"

"I don't know. I hope not!" You and Ben are a jumble of arms and legs in the giant net. You can hardly tell which way is up!

A rustling sound draws your attention back to the ground. A group of incredibly tall women dressed in leather and animal skins step out of the trees.

They are very old, with brown, wrinkled faces and white hair hanging in braids. Across their chests are slung long, curving bows, and they carry sharp spears in their hands.

"Those aren't the medicine men I was reading about!" Ben whispers to you.

"Check out their spears," you say quietly. "They don't look too friendly!"

"Warrior Women!" Ben gasps. "I read in a comic book once that the Amazon River was named after some ancient Warrior Women. They were called ... Amazons!"

The leader of the Warrior Women steps forward. She raises a decorated spear, points it right at you, and jabs!

Quick, turn to PAGE 28.

You dig round for gold on the floor, among the jewels. You can't resist slipping a few gems into your pockets.

An emerald here, a diamond there . . .

Soon, you've forgotten all about the gold, about Zoe, about everything but filling your pockets with jewels!

You're focusing on collecting gems and day-dreaming about giving your mum a thousand carat diamond! You don't notice the walls of the cave closing in on you.

The rock formations hanging down from the ceiling fit with the ones sticking up from the floor like a huge set of teeth. And those glittering teeth are chomping down on you!

You glance up from your jewel-collecting just in time.

If you move quickly, there still may be just enough room to squeeze out the way you came. Of course, you'll have to empty your pockets of all those jewels to be sure you don't get snagged on a rock.

Then again, maybe if you lie very low on the floor between two stalagmites, you won't get crunched. Then you could keep your treasure. Finders keepers. You'll be rich!

It's your choice!

Drop the jewels and slip out to PAGE 20.
Or lay low and wait for the chamber to open again on PAGE 4.

Ben's booklet explains why you have turned into a monster. Maybe with his help, you can become human again!

"The Muglani are a tribe of medicine men—you know, witch doctors," Ben explains. "They leave this enchanted fruit out here so that people will come and be turned into strange creatures. They don't like people. The Muglani want to turn all people into animals or monsters!"

"Does it say anything about how to undo the spell?" you ask Ben in a hoarse voice.

"It says in the pamphlet that there's a legendary fruit that can undo the Muglani magic. It's called the Fireheart fruit," Ben reads from his booklet.

"I remember a tree that Mrs Wheedle showed us that had fruits that looked like little red hearts. Maybe that's the one!" you tell Ben excitedly. "Will you help me find it?"

"Of course," Ben says good-naturedly. "After all, you saved me from eating that magic banana!"

"We'd better hurry," you declare, glancing at your watch. "It's already two-twenty! We've got to be back by three or Mrs Wheedle will kill us!"

"Which direction was the tree you saw? To the left or to the right?" Ben asks.

Toss a coin! If it lands on heads, go left on PAGE 43.

If it comes up tails, go right on PAGE 103.

The creeping vines fall to either side of the statue. A hideous gargoyle carved out of gleaming white stone grins out at you. It has crazy, bulging eyes and long, sharp teeth. It looks like some kind of a mutant cat creature!

"That's really creepy," Zoe says. "It gives me the shivers just looking at it."

Then you hear something else.

It sounds like a low, deep growl.

It sounds like it's coming from the statue!

You feel a hot blast of stale-smelling air on your face. That's when you notice the bits and pieces of plaster falling away from the statue.

What's going on? you think. You shake your head and blink your eyes, but it doesn't help. The great stone beast lifts one of its clawed forepaws and slices at some vines still clumped round it. They fall in pieces to the ground!

"RUN!" Zoe screams, grabbing at you. But which way? There are two paths leading away from where you are.

Down the path on the left, you see a small pool and a waterfall. Maybe you could swim away from the beast! To the right, you see a clearing with heavy sticks and rocks.

To fight the beast with sticks and stones, run to PAGE 11.

To try your luck with the water, rush to PAGE 68.

The beast takes two steps towards you and Zoe when suddenly it gives a yelp and starts to tremble! The gargoyle starts looking less like a fierce monster and more like a scared puppy dog. It looks terrified!

Whining, and with its tail between its legs, the gargoyle backs off and runs away! You're so shocked you drop your club.

"I can't believe it!" you shout to Zoe. "What happened?"

"It looked like it was afraid of something!" Zoe exclaimed. "Maybe it can't go into direct sunlight. Or maybe it's afraid of grass!"

"Ha-ha, very funny!" you retort as you cast your eyes round the clearing. That's when you notice the wooden table you glanced at before. You get a funny feeling about it.

"Maybe the gargoyle was afraid of this table," you wonder aloud as you stroll over to the ancient table.

"What's so scary about a table?" Zoe asks sarcastically, pushing her heavy brown fringe out of her eyes.

"I don't know." You shrug. You bend down to examine the enormous wooden table. That's when you realize that the table is decorated with shrunken heads!

Shrunken *human* heads!

Race to PAGE 110.

"Run!" Ben screams. "The dragon is after you!"

Quickly, you slip the pulpy Fireheart fruit into your pocket.

Ben bounds down the tunnel, heading for the exit.

You turn to run away from the dragon, but your feet slip on the rock and you hit the ground. Your breath is knocked out of you, but even worse, your club rolls away from you!

The dragon lets out an angry roar and pounces on you. The weight of the dragon pins you to the ground.

HISS! You're face to face with a deadly dragon!

Turn to PAGE 133 before it's too late!

You decide you might as well try talking to the Muglani. If you run away, he might put another spell on you.

"Excuse me, sir," you say, stepping away so that you can look him in the eye. "Are you one of the medicine men who turned me into a monster?"

"Yes, I am," he replies in a thick accent. Still you're quite amazed that this ancient tribe speaks English.

"And you've done very well. Both of you have done very well," the mysterious medicine man adds, and smiles at you.

"What do you mean?" Ben asks.

"You've found the Fireheart tree! You've passed the test!" the Muglani declares. Out of the jungle all around you, other Muglani step forward. Some of them are men, some of them are women, some are even kids. All of them wear leopard-skin robes and carry sceptres.

"We arranged the whole thing!" the Muglani explains. "We used magic to create the Junior Explorer Adventure Club and we made sure that you both found your way into the clearing with the magic fruit at the same time!"

"You mean it was all a test?" you ask.

"Yes," the medicine man chuckles. "And you won!"

"But what exactly did we win?" Ben asks nervously.

Turn to PAGE 99 to find out.

You stare into the crazy bulging eyes of the stone creature. It looks a little like a Chinese parade dragon, you think. It's baring its teeth at you in a hideous grin. You've got to make your move.

Since the beast is made of stone, it probably can't swim. There's only one catch ... Neither can you!

Desperately, you cast your eyes around. On the ground next to you, there's a big stick.

You'll definitely need something if you're going to fight off that gargoyle. Then again, maybe the stick would help you float if you jumped into the water. You pick it up.

The gargoyle swishes its tail angrily and licks its chops with its huge, gravel-coated tongue.

What's it going to be? Risk drowning or take your chances with the beast?

Better make your move before it pounces!

To fight the stone beast with the stick, turn to PAGE 112.

To jump into the water with the stick, turn to PAGE 78.

You know there's no going back. Not with that gargoyle creature outside. This cave is your only hope. But still, it's so dark and spooky in there.

"You go first, Zoe," you say as you pull yourself out on to the rocks. You gesture towards the creepy cave with one hand. "If you're so brave then you just go right ahead!"

"Okay, scaredy-cat, follow me," she says as she steps into the mouth of the cave. You stay right behind her.

You are both dripping wet and shivering. But a warm breeze is blowing through the cave. It dries you as you go.

Your eyes adjust to the darkness. Jagged rocks line the walls of the cave.

You move slowly through the dark. Zoe tells you when there's a boulder or a ditch. You walk for what seems like an eternity. Then you see something completely unexpected . . . light!

"Look!" you shout to Zoe. "That must be the way out!"

Scramble to PAGE 88.

"It's very nice of you to offer us help," you say, backing away from the Warrior Women. "But we've really got to be going."

After all, the Warrior Woman has a shrunken head in her bag. Plus, they have spears and bows and arrows. You can't trust them. They're just too dangerous!

"It was nice to meet you," Ben joins in. "See you later!"

The Warrior Woman's face turns red as you edge towards the trees. She snaps her fingers and all the Warrior Women lift their spears. And point them right at you!

You and Ben gasp in fear! A cold sweat breaks out down your spine.

"Okay," the Warrior Woman says. "I admit it. We're the ones who put that magic fruit there and turned you into a monster. We're the Muglani. And we want your heads!"

Quick, turn to PAGE 39.

54

"Let's try to swing over the tar pit!" you suggest to Ben. The Warrior Women are right behind you. There's no time to lose!

You reach for the vine, but a warm, tropical breeze picks up. It blows the vine right out of your reach.

"Hurry!" Ben cries. "The Warrior Women are coming!"

You reach further, further, trying to grasp the vine.

Hard, weathered hands clamp down on your arms.

It's too late! The Warrior Women have captured you!

Struggle to PAGE 41.

"Let's try to go round the lava," you say to Zoe.

The lava pool bubbles and hisses at you. It sends a spooky orange glow up over your face. You and Zoe step carefully to the side of the lava pool.

But your foot slips!

You flail your arms wildly! Zoe reaches out and pulls you towards her. Just in time!

You look down at the gooey, melted rubber heel of your trainer. "Gosh, thanks, Zoe," you say. "You saved my life."

"I guess you owe me big time," she says with a smile. "But we'd better keep going before those cotton-headed freaks figure out how to follow us."

The two of you make your way past the bubbling lava and through a narrow tunnel that opens into . . .

A big torchlit cavern! YOU'VE GONE IN A CIRCLE! The cave creatures cheer and laugh as they surround you again. They grab you by the arm and lead you back before King Cottonhead on his pyramid throne.

Turn to PAGE 135.

Tiny fish jaws snap shut just centimetres from your nose. Then the piranha-like fish splashes back into the water.

You take a moment to breathe deeply and check the timepiece in your pocket.

"Look!" you say, holding up the hourglass. "Our Palooka is almost up! We've got to get to that gold. And fast!"

"I know!" Zoe responds. "While I was waiting for you I tried to fish the gold out with a stick. But they ate the stick!" She holds up a short wet nub of a branch.

You cast your eyes round the cave. The walls appear to be wet. But when you examine them more closely, you see little yellow specks scattered all over the walls. They are covered with slimy little yellow slugs!

"I have an idea!" you exclaim. You pull your small army knife out of your back pocket. You unlace your shoe and tie the knife to the lace, with the blade out. Then you carefully peel one of the slugs from the wall and place it on your home-made fish hook.

"We'll go fishing!" you announce. But with bait like that, you might catch more than you bargained for.

Turn to PAGE 119 to see what you catch.

You were about to run into the clearing towards the tree. But Ben held you back just in time!

As you watch from behind the bush, Mrs Wheedle enters the clearing with the rest of the Junior Explorers right behind her.

"Hmmm," Mrs Wheedle mumbles. "I can't see the *kerritatlocus* anywhere! Where could that plant be?"

"Hey, Mrs Wheedle," Bill Green calls. "What's the name of this cool tree with all the fruit?"

"I can't remember the scientific name but here in the Amazon they call it the Fireheart tree."

You're so excited to hear that the tree actually IS the Fireheart tree that you shout out.

"Yes!" you yell.

"What was that sound?" Mrs Wheedle demands.

"It sounded like it came from over there," says Bill's little brother Fred. He points towards your hiding-place.

"What do we do now?" Ben whispers. "Should we tell them who you are? Or maybe you should just scare them away. After all, they won't recognize you!"

To step out and explain what's happened to you, go to PAGE 18.

To jump out and scare them away, go to PAGE 129.

You and Zoe race down the big tunnel.

"Where are we going to find gold?" you wonder aloud to Zoe.

"I don't know," Zoe replies. "It's not like your average scavenger hunt. Gold is pretty hard to come by!"

The tunnel is wide and well-lit by lanterns that hang from the walls about every two metres. Smaller tunnels branch off to the sides of the main tunnel.

"Quick, let's take this one." Zoe chooses. She's pointing to a tunnel that curves downwards. "There might be some gold deeper down towards the centre of the earth."

Above you, you see a tunnel that goes straight up. There's a ladder cut into the stone.

Want to take the tunnel that goes down? Turn to PAGE 14.

Want to take the ladder above you instead? Climb to PAGE 98.

"Hii-yaa!" you shout, bounding up on to the skull of the nearest tiger. Your trainer barely touches his decrepit skull, when the whole skeleton collapses to the ground.

CRASH!

You land in a tangled heap of tiger bones. Ouch! It feels like you've twisted your leg. And you can't move your arm.

The other tiger pounces on you, but since you now know how flimsy they are, you kick its skeleton to pieces with one blow of your good leg.

You won't have to worry about those tigers any more. But getting out of the pit is another story.

Your arm is turning numb and your leg feels like somebody is holding a blowtorch to it. You aren't going anywhere!

You yell for help. But by the time somebody finds you, it'll be hard to tell your bones from the tigers'.

Make no bones about it, this is

THE END.

"Please help me dig my leg out, Ben!" you shout. "If we try to drown them it could just make them angrier."

"Okay," Ben answers. He picks up the stick on the ground, kneels down carefully, and prods the anthill.

As Ben digs, the ants scurry to and fro. They're bright red with tiny pincers. You stare and stare at them.

You're feeling very hungry all of a sudden.

Before you can stop yourself, your tongue shoots out! Your tongue is huge, long and sticky! It zaps up a whole mouthful of the red ants.

CRUNCH! They taste delicious.

Ben stares up at you in amazement.

"Wow!" he exclaims. "That's some tongue!"

SPLAT! Your tongue darts out again. The ants stick to it by the hundreds. Soon you've eaten all of them!

You pull your foot out of the ruined anthill.

"I suppose I was hungry!" you tell Ben, wiping the law few ant crumbs off your mouth.

"That was gross!" Ben exclaims. "But we'd better get going. We only have a half-hour before Mrs Wheedle and the rest of the group take off for the new camp-site! We've got to find that Fireheart tree before then!"

Turn to PAGE 24.

There is one huge fish left in the pool with the hunk of gold. The giant piranha is tearing through the pool with your makeshift fishing line streaming from his mouth.

"Check out the size of that guy!" you exclaim.

"He's enormous," Zoe agrees.

You grab at your shoelace and yank the huge fish out of the water. Holding it away from your body, you set it down on the cave floor. The knife juts through its cheek.

Zoe is wading through the empty pool, reaching for the gold, when you hear a tiny gasping voice.

"Set me free," it says. The piranha is talking to you!

"If you throw me back into the pond I'll give you a wish," the fish burbles through its gaping mouth.

"This fish is talking!" you exclaim to Zoe. You almost don't believe it yourself.

"Come on. We don't have time for that!" Zoe shouts, grabbing the gold. "We've got to make it back to the king. We have the gold he asked for! Just leave the fish and let's go!"

To toss the fish back in the pond and make a wish, turn to PAGE 105.

To race for the throne chamber instead, turn to PAGE 130.

The Warrior Women lead you through the jungle to find the Fireheart fruit. Even though they seem ancient, the Warrior Women walk fast! They slip through the jungle gracefully, hardly disturbing a single leaf.

As you hike behind the Warrior Women you begin to feel very hungry. Even though you just ate that pear, you feel as if you haven't eaten in days. Maybe monsters get hungry faster than normal people.

Your stomach erupts with a loud growl. The jungle leaves begin to blur before your eyes. You're feeling faint! You've got to have some food soon!

Is that an orange tree you see off to the side of the path? It sure is! Wow! An orange would really hit the spot!

The oranges smell great! But you remember that the last time you ate a piece of fruit it turned you into a monster with bulging black eyes and gooey grey flesh.

These fruits can't be magic! you assure yourself. They're growing on a tree in the middle of the jungle! They must be safe! Your stomach growls at you. Grab an orange!

Or maybe you could ask the Warrior Women for something to eat.

To grab an orange, turn to PAGE 69.
To ask the Warrior Women for something to eat, turn to PAGE 5.

From every corner of the room, from each crevice, dark forms step out of the shadows. They move in, circling round you. Some of them are shorter than you, some taller.

And as they step into the torchlight, you realize with a chill that pierces you to the bone, there's something very un-human about them!

The first thing you notice is their bizarre heads. They look like hideous puff balls! They're perfectly round and covered in a slimy white fuzz, like moss. Their eyes are big gelatinous blobs, glossy and white!

You're almost too disgusted by their heads to notice, but their bodies are covered with heavy, grey rocklike scales instead of skin! As if someone had dipped them in glue and rolled them in a gravel pit.

What are they? Some forgotten race of cave people? With big, blobby eyes to help them see in the dark? Maybe that's what happens to you if you spend too much time underground! you think.

They are moving in on you and Zoe. Your knees are starting to feel shaky as they draw nearer.

Are they friends or enemies? Rush to PAGE 91!

"Oh, Mrs Wheedle," Zoe calls out. The group comes to a halt. "What was the name of that extremely rare flower you were describing this morning? The one that all the famous scientists are searching for?"

"Which one? You mean the *Amaryllis kerritatlocus*?"

"Is that the one with the weird twisting orange petals and the blue stems?" Zoe asks innocently.

"Yes, indeed," Mrs Wheedle answers. She starts to wring her fingers excitedly. "What about the *kerritatlocus*?"

"I've seen it!" Zoe nearly shouts. "I really have!"

"Where? WHERE?" Mrs Wheedle does a happy little jump

"I think it was over there," Zoe says, pointing back down the path. "Or maybe it was that way . . ." she says, pointing to the left of the group.

"We should split up and search for it!" you suggest.

All the kids start talking at once. Now's your chance to sneak away!

Quick! Sneak over to PAGE 42.

You chew on the pear that you took from the basket on the table. It's delicious—cool and sweet. The pear juice dribbles down your chin.

"I can't believe you did that!" Zoe's a little crazed. "You don't know where the fruit came from. It could be poisoned or something! Maybe all these people ate the fruit!" She gestures to the shrunken heads.

"I couldn't help myself," you explain, taking another greedy mouthful. "It smells so good. I couldn't resist. I don't think it's poisoned," you assure her. "It tastes too good to be poisoned."

But only moments after you've swallowed the second pulpy mouthful of pear, you start to feel dizzy.

The ground begins to twist under your feet. The trees loom over you, casting twirling shadows down on you. The leaves on the trees are doing pirouettes.

Zoe's face is spinning, spinning, spinning . . .

"What's happening to you?" You hear her desperate cry.

Spin to PAGE 94.

The dragon is behind the Fireheart tree, cowering. You race to the exit of the tunnel.

As you run, you feel the webbed hood round your head fold up and collapse back against your scaly neck and back. You never even knew you had it until you needed it.

"Ben!" you call. "Are you okay?"

"You made it!" he yells. "I can't believe it! I thought you were a goner for sure!"

"Nope, I scared the dragon! I outscared it! And look, I have the Fireheart fruit!"

The fruit is still pulsing in your hand. You stare at it, glad that it didn't get squished during the battle. Its blood-red skin is shiny and slippery.

"Here goes nothing," you say, sinking your teeth into the warm fruit.

Find out what happens next on PAGE 96.

"Run for it, Ben!" you shout. You duck out from under the medicine man's hand.

"*Uomlacka sacka!*" the medicine man commands in a foreign language. A wind whips up immediately.

"*Koo boot a lunga!*" he shouts. Eight other medicine men dressed in silver robes appear from thin air! They all look exactly like the first one. With stripes on their faces and big feathery hats. They must be some sort of magical clones! Snarling in anger, the medicine men chase you.

Ben races one way, you go another. Four of the clones chase you as you rip through the jungle. You hurtle over roots and small plants. You dodge low vines and tree branches.

You reach the banks of a river. Water rushes by in a muddy torrent. Several thick, strong vines hang down from a giant tree.

The medicine men spring out on to the bank of the river. They chuckle an evil laugh in unison. All at once, they raise their hands to grab you.

You grab one of the vines to swing over the river. You hope they're as sturdy as they look!

Swoosh over to PAGE 85.

68

You race towards the waterfall. Maybe you can lose the giant gargoyle that way. The stone beast chasing you looks a bit like a cat, you think. And cats hate water, right?

Down the path, a small pool of water is surrounded by lush tropical plants and flowers. From sixteen metres above, a river cascades down into the pool, sending up a thick mist.

"Jump into the water!" Zoe shouts. She does a perfect cannon-ball from the mossy bank.

You glance round. The stone beast appears on the path behind you. Its hideous jaws snap wildly at the air. Its thick stone leg muscles are bunched up, ready to pounce.

Turn to PAGE 51.

You decide you don't want to slow everyone down by asking them for something to eat. You'll just quickly snatch an orange.

You step into the shade of the orange tree to pluck a fruit. And find the ground under your feet has disappeared!

With a lunge you grab for the ledge.

Your knuckles scrape on small rocks buried in the soft ground. You plummet downwards!

Your arms wheel through the air. You take a nosedive, landing with a PLOP!

You're in some kind of a pit.

Steep, square walls go up about five metres. Beyond the pit you can see the deep green leaves of the jungle and the blue sky beyond them.

"Hello!" you call to Ben and the Warrior Women. "Can you hear me? I've fallen into a pit! Help me!"

But there's no sound from above. They're too far away to hear you. If only they didn't walk so quickly!

Now you're trapped!

Turn to PAGE 80.

The king stoops down, bringing his face right up to yours. He places a rocky hand on your shoulder and gazes into your eyes.

"Did you go into my treasured jewel cave?" he asks you gravely.

"What is he talking about?" Zoe asks you.

Tell the truth. Did you go into the jewelled chamber or not?

If you did go into the jewelled cave, turn to PAGE 123.

If you don't even know what the king is talking about, turn to PAGE 106.

In Cronby's tiny fist are two little nuggets of shimmering gold! Wow! If you could get them from the troll you'd be more than half-way home.

"I'll play you for the gold," Cronby bargains.

"Play what?"

"Well, since you're not scared of anything, I'll ask you a question about something really scary. If you get the question right, you get the gold and I'll show you where your friend is." So he *does* know about Zoe!

"What if I get the question wrong?" you ask.

"Well, then I get to keep the gold and your friend." The troll has an evil glint in his eye. "You see, I like to eat human beings. They're so chewy! If you lose, you have to help me carry Zoe to my kitchen. She's too heavy for me to carry by myself." He giggles in anticipation.

"No way!" you shout. You'd never bet on your best friend's life.

"But I'm afraid you have no choice!" the troll whispers. "How will you save her? You don't even know where she is!" Cronby throws his head back and laughs.

The troll is right. You must play.

Go to PAGE 15 to decide your fate ... and Zoe's!

It's an alligator! This jungle river is swarming with them. The alligator tugs you down to the river bottom. Its teeth are clamped down around your leg. As hard as you kick and wrestle, you can't shake it loose.

Strangely, it doesn't really hurt, but you are starting to get angry. You flip the gator over and bite it on the neck. After all, you have a full set of sharp monster teeth!

Immediately, the alligator lets go of you and swims away.

Yes! You just fought off an alligator!

The kids at school will never believe that one! Now all you've got to do is get back to school so you can tell them!

It's time to go and straighten all of this out. You are sure that once Mrs Wheedle and the others realize who you are they will help you work out how to turn back into a human. The answer must lie on that table with the fruit!

In a couple of deft strokes, you reach the shore of the river. You pull yourself out of the water and stand on the shore.

Gasp! Your gills huff and puff uselessly. Your eyes sting! You can't breathe!

You're suffocating!

Quick! Flip to PAGE 35.

"Oh, no!" you and Zoe scream together as you slide down the smooth stone slide.

BUMP! You land on the tunnel floor. Back where you started.

"Great!" Zoe says rolling her eyes. "We were almost out!"

"Sorry," you say. "At least the hourglass is still okay!"

You hold it up for her to see.

"Come on," she moans. "We've got to find the gold for the king—and fast!"

"Zoe," you say, "I am really sorry."

"Don't worry!" she replies. And you know that she's such a good friend she won't mention it again. "Time is running out," Zoe says. "Which way should we go?"

Turn to PAGE 14.

"The little sister is called 'Tara the Terrible'!" you declare with pride.

"ARRRRGH!" The troll jumps up and down. "I can't believe it! You've got it right again!"

You jump into the air! You did it!

"Hand over my gold!" you command Cronby.

With tears in his eyes, Cronby withdraws three fat nuggets of gold from the pocket of his little trousers and hands them over to you.

"Now show me where Zoe is!" you direct. You check the timepiece—you still have about a fifth of a Palooka left. You follow him to the mouth of the tunnel, where Zoe is sitting, all tied up. Cronby unties her and scurries away.

"I've got our gold!" you exclaim.

"All right!" She gives you a high five. "How did you do it?" You tell her the whole story on your way to the pyramid.

You and Zoe reach the grand chamber as the last few grains of sand are about to fall through the hourglass.

"We've got the gold!" you shout triumphantly.

The king himself shows you out into the jungle. You safely meet up with the Junior Explorer Adventure Club.

And what an adventure it was!

THE END

The bubbling tar pit isn't that wide. Maybe you can make it if you hurdle towards the other bank.

"Jump for it!" you shout to Ben.

You take a flying leap for the other side.

You almost make it. Your feet slip on the far bank of the pit. Your feet slide into the steaming tar. You fall backwards, arching through the air.

SPLAT! The sticky tar covers you from head to toe.

SPLAT! Ben lands right on top of you.

The more you struggle, the deeper you sink.

Looks like you're stuck . . . for good.

THE END

"What is it? Why do you have to go back?" Zoe asks. She stops climbing and glances down at you over her shoulder. "We're almost free!"

"I still have the king's timepiece!" you moan. "I can't steal it. That wouldn't be right!"

"Listen," Zoe says impatiently. "Just set it down over there. He'll find it sooner or later." She points at a big rock sticking out of the side of the tunnel. The rock is flat on top, just like a shelf. It looks as if the timepiece would fit right on the rock.

"Anyway," Zoe continues, checking her big watch, "the rest of our group will be hiking out of here at three o'clock. It's two-twenty-five! We've only got about half an hour left before they leave!"

"I feel bad," you moan. "He said it meant a lot to him. I should set it down in the tunnel or something."

"That king was so mean to us. I can't believe you feel sorry for him! If it were me," Zoe says, "I'd keep the hourglass and sell it for a lot of money!"

Time's a-wasting. What are you going to do?

If you rest it on the shelf, go to PAGE 128.
If you keep it, go to PAGE 9.

You are surrounded by the strange medicine men.

"I'm sorry," you apologize. "It's not that we don't think it would be really cool to join you all. It's just that we have families waiting for us."

"Yeah," Ben joins in. "They would really miss us if we became medicine men."

"We understand," the tall Muglani says. "But you also have to understand that we can't have you blabbing about all of our secrets." He rubs his sceptre between his palms slowly.

"We promise we won't tell anyone!" you declare.

"Well, we really should go," Ben adds. "Bye!"

You turn your backs on the Muglani to leave.

"Oom oom oom Klak-kwe-vod-rup!" you hear behind you.

You feel your body changing again. This time brown hair pushes out through your skin—all over your body. You start shrinking, too! And grow a tail!

You're a monkey! And next to you is another monkey wearing tiny glasses. It's Ben!

When the Muglani said he didn't want you telling their secrets, he really meant it! Well, at least you have a friend to monkey around with. You two can really go bananas!

THE END

Just as the gargoyle pounces at you, you do a clumsy backward dive off the bank into the water.

You plunge down into the deep pool, gripping the heavy stick with both hands. It seems as if you're underwater for too long, but then . . .

Your face and arms break the surface and you can breathe again. The stick floats! Thank goodness!

"You made it!" Zoe cheers.

"Yeah!" you cry in triumph, gasping for air. The water is icy cold. It's like taking a bath in an ice-cube tray!

"Look!" Zoe says breathlessly. She points to the shore. The stone beast is prowling to and fro on the bank. It looks angry. "It won't come near the water," Zoe declares.

"Excellent!" you say, shivering. "But what do we do now? If we stay in here much longer, I think I'll freeze to death. I'm already starting to lose the feeling in my toes!"

Zoe doesn't say anything. Her teeth are chattering too hard. You feel your feet beginning to grow numb from the freezing water. Are you destined to become two human ice-cubes? Or will you be torn apart by a big walking rock?

Dog-paddle over to PAGE 6 to find out if you have any hope.

"Don't eat it!" you shout to Ben as he lifts the banana to his mouth. He has an odd, dreamy expression on his face. You step up to him and knock the banana from his hand.

At first, Ben looks furious that you smashed the banana away from him. His face turns red.

Then he looks puzzled and shakes his head. As if he were waking from a dream.

"Thank you!" Ben says. "You broke the spell!"

"What spell?" you manage to croak. "What are you talking about?"

"This fruit is enchanted! It was left here by a tribe of medicine men. It is all explained in this pamphlet I got at the hotel! It's called 'The Myth of the Muglani'."

Go to PAGE 46 to find out more about the "Muglani".

80

You stand with your hands on your hips and examine the pit. Now how am I going to get out of this pit? you think. And why would someone dig a big hole in the middle of the jungle, anyway?

You take two steps back. Maybe you can jump up and get a handhold on the bank of the pit.

As your foot lands you hear a loud CRUNCH!

And the CRUNCH extends into a ghostly RATTLE.

The sound makes the hairs on the back of your neck prickle. A spooky breeze sweeps over you.

There is something moving behind you!

It sounds as if it might be a bunch of old bones.

You turn round very slowly and very carefully.

Turn to PAGE 126.

"Nice to meet you, Cronby," you say to the troll, burying your hands in your pockets. "Have you seen my friend Zoe?"

The troll wrinkles up his brow, as if he's thinking very hard. "Is she about this tall?" he says, holding a hand up to exactly Zoe's height. "With freckles and hair in her face and not very good manners?"

"Yeah." You nod. "That sounds like her."

"Yeah," Cronby says, sticking his hands in his pockets and imitating you. "I saw which way she went."

"Where is she?" you demand.

The troll sits down on top of a small rock and crosses his legs. "I'll tell you where she went if you tell me what you're doing down here! It's not often we see human kids down here," he says with curiosity.

"To cut a long story short," you explain, "we were chased inside the waterfall and we've got to find three pieces of gold for the king or we'll be turned into slaves."

"Ooooh! You must be scared!" he whispers.

"No, I'm not scared at all," you say with confidence.

"Not scared at all, eh?" Cronby says, his red eyes glimmering. "Well, you're in luck! Look what I have here."

Flip to PAGE 71 to see what he's got.

You reach to pluck one of the Fireheart fruits. The dragon still doesn't see you. You're moving too slowly for the dragon to see!

The heat from the lava makes your eyes water. You take one of the Fireheart fruits in your grey, clawed hand.

It's warm! Just like a real heart. And the soft, fleshy fruit is pulsing with the heat of the lava, like a real heart would pulse. It feels as if you're holding someone's heart. Gross!

With a flick of your wrist, you break the fruit from the tree. You hold it carefully in your hand. You don't want to break it open with one of your sharp claws!

You turn to Ben and flash him a toothy smile.

Then you hear a violent HISS!

The dragon lunges at you from behind the tree!

Dash to PAGE 49!

"I'm not afraid to go first, Zoe!" you declare as you scramble up on to the slimy rocks.

"Oh, yeah? Prove it!" she says to you.

"There's nothing in here that can scare me!" you say bravely.

You glance back as Zoe pulls herself out of the cold water. She takes off her windcheater to wring it dry. She turns to you and flashes you a grin.

You start to make your way deeper into the cave. The walls are wet and slimy. You don't want to touch them but you have to or you'll fall. The cave air feels hot and humid. And there's the strangest warm breeze. It's almost as if someone were breathing on you!

"Weird!" you remark to Zoe. "The cave floor is pink!"

She doesn't answer you.

"Zoe?" you call. "Where are you?"

Again there's no answer. You peer into the darkness behind you. But you're all alone.

Or maybe you're not so alone after all. You have a funny feeling something is watching you . . . from *inside* the cave.

Follow your hunch to PAGE 23.

84

You and Ben scramble over the rocks and into the cave. The rocks are covered by a strange white moss. The moss glows a little, helping you to see better in the dark cave. You use your club as a walking stick. It helps you balance as you climb over the craggy stones.

"I wonder why it's so hot in here," Ben murmurs. "Usually caves are cooler than the air outside!"

"It's really boiling in here!" you agree.

As you stumble along, the tunnel begins to glow with a faint gold light. The cave grows brighter and brighter.

"I can see the tree!" you exclaim as you reach the chamber that Unger told you about.

"Wow!" Ben shouts.

There in the centre of the cave is a pool of lava. From the centre of the pool grows a beautiful little tree. Its low sweeping branches are filled with ripe red fruits. They hang like drops of blood from every branch.

"How cool is that?" you exclaim. Ben puts down his stick and gives you a high five. "We've found the Fireheart tree!"

But as you step towards the tree, you hear a low, menacing HISS!

Scramble to PAGE 10.

You have a good grip on the vine. You expect to go sailing over the river, away from all the medicine men.

But as you grasp the vine, you notice it has a strange texture. It doesn't feel like a plant. Plants don't have scales! Plants don't slither in your hand! And plants don't hiss!

Gasp! You're holding on to a giant boa constrictor!

The snake quickly loops itself round you and drops out of the tree. You drop with it!

The medicine men stand round shaking their heads sadly as the tremendous boa constrictor wraps itself round you. They wanted to shrink your head.

Too bad for them!

If they try to take you away from the boa it will have a real HISSY FIT!

THE END

"We've got to find our way out of these tunnels!" you exclaim, checking your watch.

You and Zoe have the same kind of big, clunky, waterproof watches. They are indestructible. And they come with little watch-face lights—just perfect for when you're stuck in a cave—like right now.

"It's two-forty-five!" you declare. "We've got to make it back to the Junior Explorers by three."

"Let's take this big tunnel over here." Zoe gestures towards a wide, round tunnel.

"I think we should head this way," you insist, pointing to a small burrow in a patch of soft earth near the floor of the tunnel. The hole is just big enough for you to fit through. "It looks as if some kind of animal created this hole. It could lead to the surface!"

"I know," Zoe says. "Why don't we each go and explore a little? We can cover twice as much ground that way. We'll meet up in a few minutes and report what we found."

"Great idea! We'll meet back here in five minutes." You check your indestructible watch one last time. "I have a very good feeling about this tunnel!"

You couldn't be more wrong.

Squeeze on through to PAGE 22.

"Guard dragon?" you say. "What do you mean, 'guard dragon'?"

But Unger has gone! She and the rest of the Warrior Women have disappeared into the rich foliage of the jungle.

"Well, thanks again!" Ben calls after them.

"Do you think she was serious about the guard dragon?" you ask Ben nervously.

"I don't know," Ben answers.

"Maybe we should bring in some kind of weapon, to protect ourselves from the dragon," you wonder aloud.

"What about these sticks?" Ben asks, pointing to two heavy branches lying on the ground.

"Those look perfect," you exclaim. You pick up the branches and hand one to Ben. "Well, we'd better hurry. We've only got about ten minutes before the Junior Explorers leave without us! Let's go into the cave!"

Race to PAGE 84!

Zoe speeds over the rocks towards the bright light. You hurry to keep up. You can't wait to get out of this cave and meet up with your group. Even Mrs Wheedle is sounding pretty good to you right about now.

But when you glance up, you see you have stumbled into some sort of large underground chamber. The light you saw was not from the sun. It was torchlight! Cast by hundreds of blazing torches that decorate the room you now stand in.

"Cool!" Zoe murmurs. "What *is* this place?"

The cavern is so tall you can't even see the ceiling. But the floor is covered in soft carpets! At the end of the room, a small pyramid rises.

"It looks just like the ones we studied in ancient history class!" you whisper, pointing to the pyramid.

"Yeah! But this isn't history. This is NOW. Check out that throne!" Zoe says in amazement.

At the top of the pyramid is a golden throne draped with what appear to be tiger skins. Zoe walks over to it, gaping at the splendid throne. But you're starting to feel nervous. Somebody lit all these torches and you're not so sure you want to be around when they get back.

Too late.

"Uh-oh!" Zoe whispers. "Somebody's coming!"

Who is it? Find out on PAGE 63.

The ants are frantically trying to get back in their anthill. They crawl all over your leg. And begin to bite!

"Quick, pour the water over my leg!" you cry to Ben.

A large green plastic canteen is slung over Ben's shoulder. He opens the canteen and drenches the anthill with the water.

The water doesn't kill the ants. It just makes them REALLY angry! They swarm over your leg. The bites make your leg feel as if it's on fire!

The anthill is all muddy now, and your leg is stuck even deeper than it was before.

"Ow! Ben! Help me!" you call. "Pull me out!"

Ben takes one step towards you but stops.

"I can't!" he exclaims. "I'm allergic to insect bites! I'll try to find help!" Ben takes off, running at full speed.

If only you'd turned into a gopher instead of a clumsy, bug-eyed fish monster! Then you could have dug your way out.

Because by the time Ben gets back, it will be too late.

The ants will have moved your whole body out of their anthill. Bit by bit. Bite by bite.

THE END

"It was a bat," you say with confidence.

"WRONG!" the troll screams. He's delighted. "It was a dog. I win! Now I'm going to have kid stew! And roast child! And girl casserole!"

"But I'm sure it was a bat!" you insist.

"It was not a bat!" Cronby yells. "Not a bat!"

"It was a big bat!" you insist. "A big bat!"

Cronby makes it into a little song. "Not a bat! Not a bat! Not a bat!" His voice gets louder and louder, rising in pitch until it's a screech.

As he sings his awful song, another sound fills the tunnel as well. It's a fluttering sound, a whoosh!

Cronby's screeches fade away as the flapping gets louder and louder. A giant, hairy bat lands on top of the boulder!

Quick, flip to PAGE 17.

What do these bizarre cave people want from you? you wonder as they come closer and closer.

"Look up there!" Zoe yells. She points to the pyramid.

All the creatures fall to their knees suddenly.

A huge figure appears on the throne at the top of the pyramid. He must be over three metres tall. His face is covered with strange slimy moss, like the others, but it is gold-coloured, not white, and huge horns stick out of each side of his big spongy head. He wears a robe of animal skins.

"Greetings," he booms.

He speaks English!

The cave creatures draw towards you. Maybe they just want to say hello, like their king. Then again, why are they surrounding you if they are friendly? In a flash, you scan the cavern for an escape route. They are all around you . . .

But off to your left there seems to be a gap!

If you make a break for it now, you just might get away from them.

Or you could stay and hear what the big king has to say. Who knows, he could be nice . . . possibly.

It's your choice.

To make a run for it, race to PAGE 131.
To hear the king out, turn to PAGE 107.

You strain to see what is in the room with you. Slowly your eyes adjust to the dimness.

BANG! The cave creatures are still trying to get in!

You see a face ahead of you! It's . . . Zoe. Or at least Zoe's reflection. And it's broken up into a thousand little pieces. Like you're gazing into one of those mirrored balls.

BANG! CRACK! The creatures are breaking down the door!

You see your own reflection, too. A thousand times over. Weird, you think. What is it? Then you freak out as you realize what it is you're staring at . . . the eye of a spider. A giant burrowing tarantula to be exact!

The door bursts open and the creatures rush in.

"Look out!" they cry. "Be careful!"

You turn back to the giant spider. It's covered with thick brown hairs. Its pincers snap open and closed. The spider looks hungry! You take three steps towards the door. But it's too late. With one sweep of its long, hairy forelegs, the spider gathers you and Zoe up. It wraps you in thick strands of silk.

"We tried to warn you!" the cave creatures say sadly.

You want to say "thanks anyway" but you're a bit busy. In fact, you're really tied up. Because this is the bitter

END.

You take the tunnel to the left and run like crazy.

Oh no! Your trainer is untied. You step on the lace and find yourself flying . . . flying . . . flying . . . through the air.

CRUNCH! You land in a heap on the floor.

The ant drops the boulder to the ground. It skitters up to you and gingerly places one of its six feet on your body.

With a press of its heel, it smushes you.

The last thing you hear is the ant saying, "Eww! I hate these pink bugs! I've got to call the exterminator!"

Yuck! You have come to a very messy

END.

"Can you hear me? Are you okay?" Zoe asks anxiously, leaning over you. You've fallen to the ground. The pear rolled out of your hand and is sitting in the grass.

It feels as if a bomb has gone off inside your head. Your whole body feels sore and a little tingly.

"I think I'm okay," you say to Zoe. But instead of words, what comes out is a blubbery howl!

"Oh, no!" Zoe cries in horror. "I can't believe it!"

Her eyes look as if they might pop out of her head. She is pale and trembling.

You move towards her. You want to tell her everything is okay. But she backs away.

And then Zoe—your best friend in the whole world—turns away from you and runs, screaming, into the jungle!

"Zoe, wait!" you try to call out. But you just make more disgusting bleating sounds. Your throat is filled with some kind of goo that keeps you from speaking clearly.

Why would she run away like that? you wonder. She looked really scared, as if you were a monster or something!

That's when you see your hands. And let out a scream of your own.

Your skin has changed!

Find out how on PAGE 136.

The Warrior Woman finishes looking you over and stands up.

"She's got a shrunken head in her bag," you whisper to Ben.

"Maybe they are the Muglani after all!" Ben whispers back.

"Listen, my friends!" the head Warrior Woman says in perfect English.

"The Muglani have struck again! We've got to help these kids reverse the spell of those terrible Muglani.

"My name is Unger," the Warrior Woman announces to you and Ben. She puts out her hand and helps you both to your feet. "The Muglani are our enemies. We always try to help the unfortunate people that the Muglani turn into monsters. Will you accept our help?"

Unger extends her hand for you to shake. You see the shrunken head peeping out of her bag. Hmmmm . . .

Can you really trust these strange women or should you go on your own way? You see by your watch it's already two-thirty. You've got no time to lose!

To accept their help, turn to PAGE 122.
To turn down the offer and go on your way, turn to PAGE 53.

Wow! The Fireheart fruit has a wonderful flavour. It's like a strawberry cake.

As you chew, your skin begins to tingle. Your face twitches and jumps. The jungle spins. Everything blurs together and twirls faster and faster. BANG! It all stops!

You take your hands away from your face.

"It worked!" Ben exclaims. "You're a kid again!"

You did it! Ben thumps you on the back and you burp.

You burp up a little fire!

You and Ben race back towards the path where the Junior Explorers were. It doesn't take you long to find the group. Mrs Wheedle is shouting for everyone to get in line for a head count. Whew! Just in time!

Zoe's there. And she's really glad to see you. She apologizes for running from you the way she did.

"No sweat," you tell her. "Ben and I will tell you the whole story!"

When you get back home, you become famous for your fire burps. You're booked on all the late-night talk shows. It's also very handy for roasting marshmallows for your two best friends, Zoe and Ben.

THE END

The cave creatures pull you between them.

"This is not a tug-of-war!" you shout. "Let go of me!"

A flash of light bursts from near by and the creatures instantly drop you! They moan in pain, covering their eyes.

The bright light seems to be hurting their eyes. What is it? you wonder. Then you see Zoe standing there, grinning from ear to ear. She's holding a powerful mini-torch.

"I completely forgot I had this!" Zoe exclaims. "Quick, let's get out of here once and for all!"

You make your way back through the waterfall. The gargoyle has given up guarding the pool, so you are able to rejoin the Junior Explorers. They almost left without you!

Later that night, you and Zoe sit in your tent discussing your adventures. You suddenly remember that you still have the king's timepiece. You reach into your shirt pocket to show Zoe.

To your surprise, you find the hourglass *and* a handful of gems! They must have landed in your pockets when the jewel chamber crunched down and sprayed you with rocks.

You split the sparkling emeralds, rubies, sapphires and diamonds with Zoe fifty-fifty. Forget about being Junior Explorers. Now you're Junior Millionaires!

THE END

98

"Zoe," you call. "Let's take this one that goes up! It might even lead to the surface!"

"Yeah," she agrees. "Then we could just go back to the Junior Explorers and forget about this whole thing!"

"That would be great!" you say. "Here, I'll boost you up."

Once Zoe's up on the ladder, you scramble up on some loose rocks. Up the ladder, you climb and climb and climb.

The tunnel gets brighter as you climb. You're almost back in the jungle! Soon you can smell the flowers. You can even hear the tropical birds singing to each other.

"We're almost out," Zoe announces.

"Wow!" you add. "I can't believe it was so easy!"

But then you remember . . . something awful!

"Zoe," you whisper gravely, "I have to go back!"

Oh, no! Tell Zoe why on PAGE 76.

The head medicine man waves his sceptre in the air majestically. "By finding the Fireheart tree together, you have passed the test!" He reaches into a pocket and withdraws a handful of some kind of powder. He sprinkles the powder over your head.

It tingles! You feel your skin change back to human skin! The claws disappear. Your sharp teeth return to normal. You're a kid again!

"Since you've passed the test, we will now make you both Muglani of the Amazon!" His voice booms through the jungle. He claps his hands slowly. Soon all the Muglani join in clapping. They begin to chant. *"Oom oom oom mah-hek-nee-hay."*

"Do you want to be a medicine man?" you whisper to Ben.

"No, do you?" he asks. You shake your head. The Muglani aren't paying attention to you. They're all busy clapping and chanting.

"Excuse me!" you interrupt. Silence fills the air as the Muglani stare at you. "But we don't WANT to be Muglani!"

"We'll just see about that!" the head Muglani says with an evil smile.

Jump to PAGE 77.

100

Right in the centre of the pool is a nugget of gold as big as your fist!

Not only that, but behind the pool you can see the main tunnel that leads right to the throne chamber. All you've got to do is grab the gold and race back to the king.

"Cool!" you exclaim. "Let's grab it and get this over with!" You reach your hand out to snatch the gold from the pool.

Snap! A fish jumps out of the water and nearly bites off your finger with its razor-sharp teeth.

"What was that?" you cry. You bend over the water for a look.

A hundred or more fish are swimming in the pool. They have blind white eyes and sharp teeth that stick out of their mouths like pin-cushions. Their skin is clear, too. You can see their insides as they thrash around.

"Get back!" Zoe screams as another fish flies out of the water right at your face!

Step back to PAGE 56!

You race through the jungle at an amazing speed. Your legs are suddenly stronger than ever before! You can also see much better than before. It's probably because your eyes are so big!

The hunters are right on your trail. BANG! A bullet whizzes through the air. They're shooting at you!

You've got to get away. To the left, you see a big flower hidden by heavy vines. You could hide in it. Or you could keep running. You're not sure how you know it, but some weird new sense you have tells you that there's water ahead!

To run to the water, turn to PAGE 108.

To hide inside the huge flower, turn to PAGE 16.

102

"Oh, no!" you cry. "It can't be!"

The stone people are closing in fast and you're stuck on a ledge in front of a pool of molten lava.

You've reached the centre of a volcano!

"What are we going to do?" Zoe asks, grabbing your arm. Panic is in her eyes.

"We could try to fight them," you suggest. "Maybe they're not as tough as they look."

The cave creatures are approaching slowly. They are watching to see what you'll do. Sweat is washing down your face and neck. You glance round the hot cave, looking for options. You see that behind the lava pool the tunnel continues.

"Maybe we could try to get round the edge of the pool," you offer.

"It seems pretty dangerous," Zoe says. Bubbles of scalding air pop at the surface of the pool of fiery red-and-orange molten rock.

"Yeah, but so do they," you answer, nodding towards the angry cave creatures.

If you fight the cave people, battle over to PAGE 19.

If you try to work your way round the edge of the lava pool instead, go round to PAGE 55.

"I think the tree was this way," you say, turning to the right. "I hope we can find it in time!"

You lead Ben through the dense jungle. The air is hot and damp. Soon you're soaked with sticky sweat. Your new monster skin is gross and gooey. It even starts to stick to the leaves as you part them with your webbed fingers.

You take a step to go round a huge rubber-tree plant when one of the broad, shiny leaves bounces right into your face. It sticks to your skin, blinding you.

You stumble forwards.

"Look out!" Ben cries. "Watch your feet!"

It's too late! You feel your foot sink down into some kind of hole.

Sink on down to PAGE 27.

Where could Zoe have gone? The tunnel is a dead end. There's no way out and you were right behind her!

"Zoe?" you call. "Zoe! Where are you?"

Where are you? you? you? you? your voice echoes back.

That's when you notice the tip of a shoe sticking out from behind a boulder over to your left. It's a green shoe. The tip of it curves upward . . . like an elf's shoe.

"Who's there?" you demand.

Turn to PAGE 26, quick.

"But wait, Zoe, I could wish for more time!" you say, stooping to pick up the slimy piranha. It's so slippery it nearly drops out of your hands before you can get the hook out.

"You are SO right!" Zoe exclaims, spinning round. "We can wish ourselves right out of this mess!" She steps back out of the pool.

"There you go," you murmur as you ease the fish back into the water.

The fish opens his mouth and a few bubbles escape. As the bubbles break on the surface, his words drift up to you.

"What is it you wish for?"

"I want to be out of this mess," you nearly shout. "Take us back to our school group, up in the jungle."

The fish opens its mouth and a huge silver bubble pops up to the surface ... The word "GRANTED!" echoes through the cave.

Your head is filling with silver light. It spreads throughout your whole body.

Flash! Fly to PAGE 8.

"Your Majesty." You address the king. "I can honestly say I did not go into your jewel chamber."

"I believe you," the king says to you. Then he straightens up and speaks to all the cave dwellers.

"Three cheers for the humans!"

The cave creatures shout, "Hip-hip-hooray!" They lift you down from the pyramid and carry you round on their scaly shoulders.

You grin at Zoe as the cave people carry you round the cavern. They place you down in front of a long table. Platters of rich and exotic food are stacked on the table.

You realize sometime during the feast that you were supposed to rejoin your school group back in the jungle.

But there's something about these cave dwellers that makes you want to stick around. Maybe for ever.

It could be their cute fuzzy faces, or their pretty glassy eyes. Or maybe it's the magic "enslavement" powder they sprinkled on your food.

You and Zoe live with the cave people for so long that you don't even mind when moss grows on your face and your eyes turn to jelly!

You're just one of the gang, fuzz face!

THE END

You decide to hear what the king has to say.

"Maybe the king will show us a way out," you whisper to Zoe.

"Humans!" his voice booms through the cavern. "Come forward!"

Two of the rock people grab you, one on each arm. Their hands are covered in stone chips. The stones dig into your skin.

"Ow!" you exclaim.

"Let us go," Zoe cries.

The rock people drag you both up to the top of the pyramid. They throw you down at the king's feet. Maybe you should have run when you had the chance!

Turn to PAGE 135.

108

You can sense that you are near water, so you keep running. Bullets rip through the leaves all around you.

BANG! BANG!

A beach! You leap out of the heavy foliage of the jungle on to the banks of a swift river.

"Oh, no!" Gwen Shripp cries. "Don't let it get to the water!"

The bullets whiz at you from every direction. You kick off your trainers and dive into the water. Your feet are webbed, too! You can swim incredibly well.

You cut through the water away from Gwen Shripp, the world-famous hunter. The river is cold but it feels wonderful on your gooey skin. Your gigantic eyes immediately adjust to the darkness of the muddy river. You realize you can breathe underwater! The cool water flows through the gills on the side of your head.

For the first time since you bit that strange fruit, all is calm and quiet around you. But not for long . . .

SNAP! From behind you, a set of teeth clamps down on your leg! You cry out in surprise! What now?

Turn to PAGE 72.

"Let's head that way," you remark to Zoe. "Since there are so many little tunnels we'll have a better chance of finding the gold."

"Excellent," she agrees.

You enter the tunnel. Small tunnels branch off like spokes on a wheel, or a giant spider's web.

"Let's split up," Zoe offers. "We'll meet back here in five minutes."

"Okay," you agree. You both check the time on your watches. "And if either of us gets lost, we'll just call out to each other!"

"You got it!" Zoe scrambles into a small tunnel to the left.

You've only stepped a few paces into a different tunnel when you hear a heavy thud behind you.

When you turn round your mouth drops open in shock. You see two long pointed feelers waving through the air.

Your eyes are nearly popping out of your head.

Scraping the top of the tunnel is a huge boulder held up by two big, black pincers. The pincers belong to a giant ant! And it's running at you.

Full speed!

Quick, bolt to PAGE 132.

"Zoe!" you yell. "There are shrunken heads on this table!"

"Let me see!" Zoe bends down next to you.

The table is made out of old, cracked wood. A basket on the tabletop overflows with bananas, oranges and pears.

The little heads hang off the tabletop by red strings. Their skin is wrinkled and yellow—almost like old, dried-up apples. Each head has a surprised expression on its tiny face.

"Too creepy!" Zoe exclaims. "Let's not stick around."

"I agree," you say. "I wanted to have an adventure, but having my head shrunk wasn't exactly what I had in mind . . ." You start to stand up and walk away from the strange table when you smell something delicious. It smells fantastic!

"What's that smell?" you ask Zoe.

"It's the weird fruit in that basket," she replies.

You turn back to the table. The fruit smells so good, you can't believe it. It's the most wonderful scent you've ever smelled in your life. Your mouth starts to water. You can almost taste the sugary flavour of fruit upon your tongue.

You have to have some of that fruit. You don't care what else you do, you have to taste that fruit.

You reach out with your hand and pick up a beautiful green pear. You sink your teeth into it.

Quick! Turn to PAGE 65.

You turn quickly. A tall man is standing behind you! He's wearing a robe of leopard skins and carries a big stick in one hand. His face is painted with stripes. And he has a big feathery hat, just like the witch doctors you've seen in movies!

The Muglani places a heavy hand on your shoulder.

Your mind races. What should you do? The Muglani doesn't have a very good grip on you. You could wriggle out of his grasp and run away. Or you could try to reason with him. He doesn't look very dangerous.

To escape from the Muglani, slip away to PAGE 67.

To reason with him, proceed to PAGE 50.

"GRRRRRR!" The stone creature opens its mouth to roar. You see rows and rows of white stone teeth like sharp rocks.

You tighten your grip on the stick and prepare to fight.

"Don't be crazy!" Zoe shouts from the pool. "He's much too big for you ..."

Too late for that now. The gargoyle pounces, flying through the air.

RRRRRRRIP! Its cold, stone claws tear through the material of your shirt as it pushes you down.

The stone beast pins you to the ground by your shoulders. It sticks out its tongue and licks your face!

"AAAAHHHH!" You scream in pain as the rough surface of its tongue scrapes across your cheek ... over and over and over again.

Looks like he's got you licked ...

THE END

I'd better get Zoe now! you think to yourself. It would be terrible to leave your friend stuck in the mountain.

You crawl into the damp earthen tunnel again. You have dirt crusted in your hair. It's all over your clothes. It's even in the soles of your trainers.

All of a sudden you bump into something. Something that wasn't in the tunnel before. Something soft.

You poke at it with one hand. It pushes back against you! You try to crawl backwards through the hole, but it's useless.

So that's who made this tunnel, you think. A GIANT EARTHWORM! And unfortunately, this worm is no ordinary giant earthworm. It's a carnivorous night crawler. One of the many rare species that live in the jungle.

Normal earthworms take dirt in through one end, mash it up, and squirt it out the other end.

This worm eats people! It sucks you in, mushes you up, and squirts you out the other

END.

114

"Okay," you announce. "I accept your challenge."

"Good," Cronby says. "If you get it right, I'll give you three pieces of gold and you and Zoe will go free. If you lose though," he rubs his hands together greedily, "I get to keep BOTH you and Zoe!"

Gulp!

"What's the question?" you ask. In your head you're trying to remember every GOOSE-BUMPS book you've ever read.

"Hmmmmmm . . . In a book called *The Cuckoo Clock of Doom*, there's a boy who has a little sister who's a real pain. Is her name Tara the Terrible or Tanya the Terror?"

That question IS harder . . . But you know the answer!

If you think her name was "Tara the Terrible", go to PAGE 74.

If you think it was "Tanya the Terror", go to PAGE 32.

The hunter is raising her gun towards you! You don't have a moment to lose! You jump out from beneath the table and bound into the jungle.

You're into the dense leaves and vines before the hunters can stop you. Their reflexes are slow. They're probably still shocked by the way you look! Even Gwen Shripp looks stunned. Her mouth hangs open. But only for a moment.

"Quickly! After it!" Gwen commands.

"But what IS it?" her husband asks nervously.

"It appears to be some new species of amphibian," you hear the hunter reply. "Whatever it is, I'm going to get it!"

Keep running to PAGE 101, as fast as you can!

The king gazes into Zoe's face and bellows, "If you want us to show you the way out—YOU'RE GOING TO HAVE TO EARN IT!" He lets go of her and she tumbles back to the ground next to you.

"I shall set you a task. If you can accomplish it in a certain amount of time, I will let you go free. If you cannot . . ." The king shakes his horned head sadly.

"Your Majesty, what will happen to us if we can't do it?" you ask bravely.

"I WILL KEEP YOU HERE AS MY SLAVES FOR EVER!" he roars.

All the stone people snort and giggle as if their king had just told the best joke ever.

The king claps his stony hands three times. "Bring forward the timepiece!" he commands.

Turn forward to PAGE 120.

"Row, row, row your boat," you sing.

The tigers cock their heads at you and listen. It's working!

"Gently down the stream," your voice wavers. Why can't you think of the words to any *good* songs?

As you sing, the tigers tap their paws and seem to enjoy the music. Cool! You've made friends with them.

"Okay," you say, "I'll just be going now!" You grab on to some roots sticking out of the clay wall and try to lift yourself up.

Immediately the tiger skeletons rip at the air with their claws. You jump away from their razor-sharp nails.

"Row, row, row your boat," you sing until the tigers settle down again. "Gently down the stream."

You've found two real music lovers. And you're stuck with them, for ever.

As long as you *never stop singing*, everything will go just merrily, merrily, merrily, merrily, merrily . . .

THE END

You shoot down the smooth and polished tunnel. The floor is covered by a slimy, watery moss.

You are gaining speed!

The sides of the chute are spotted with weird pink flowers growing in packs.

They have thick, fleshy petals. They look like big tongues sticking out of the wall. Gross! You do everything you can to avoid them.

Then you see the biggest of the tongue-flowers ahead of you. It hangs down in the tunnel, blocking your way.

You fly at it head first and get stuck on it!

It licks you! Yuck!

You punch and kick at the disgusting flower.

Finally you slip past it and land in a heap on the floor of a small room.

In the centre of the room is a still pool of water. Zoe is standing at the side of the pool, staring down into it.

"Took you long enough!" she jokes. "Check this out! I've found our last piece of gold! The only question is . . . how do we get it out?"

Go to PAGE 100 to find out.

"Yeah, right," Zoe mumbles, rolling her eyes. "We'll fish for piranhas! There's only about a million fish in there. It won't take any time at all!"

You ignore her sarcasm and carefully lower the makeshift fishing hook into the pool.

The piranhas swarm round it, thrashing and fighting each other. The water boils with their whipping bodies.

Then the piranhas thrash out of the water! Jumping all over you! You feel their sharp teeth on your arms and legs.

"Help me!" you cry to Zoe, brushing wildly at the deadly piranhas. Zoe slaps at the fish. One by one, they fall to the floor, flipping and thrashing round.

You knock the last one off and stand there catching your breath. The piranhas on the ground finally stop moving.

"I can't believe it!" Zoe whispers in amazement.

"I didn't think they would attack me! But it actually worked! They're dead!"

"All except for one!" Zoe remarks, pointing at the pool. "The mother of them all . . ."

Hook the big one on PAGE 61.

Four servants hurry up the steps of the pyramid with a huge golden cage. Within the cage is an enormous hourglass. They place the timepiece in front of the king.

The king points a stony finger at you and Zoe. "You must bring me three pieces of gold from inside this mountain." His voice echoes through the cavern. "You have one Palooka to find the gold."

"One WHAT?" Zoe asks.

"One Palooka!" the king answers. "It's our unit of time measurement here in the mountain."

"Pardon me, sir," you interject. "But do you know what that breaks down to in human time? Hours and minutes maybe?" You tap on your watch to show him what you're talking about.

"I don't know," the king snaps. "Here, take my pocket timepiece." He hands you a beautiful little hourglass in a silver box. It's so small it fits right in your hand.

"That was a gift from my mother," the king says, bowing his head. "If you lose it I will boil you in lava!" He doesn't look like he's joking either!

"On the count of three we will work the timepieces together. ONE . . . TWO . . .

Quick, turn to PAGE 3.

The king opens the tent flaps and sticks his head in. He sneers at you.

Your heartbeat quickens as you stare at the slimy, mossy face of the king.

How did he find you? you wonder. What's he going to do?

The hourglass in your hands feels as if it's made of ice. You try to hide it behind your back but the king sees it.

"GIVE ME MY TIMEPIECE!" he commands.

Shaking from head to foot, you pass him the beautiful little hourglass.

With a flash, the king tosses a handful of powder on you and vanishes.

Coughing, you wave your hand in the air. You are choking on the gritty dust. Choking and shivering. It's getting cold.

Very cold.

Dead cold.

Maybe it's because the king scared you so much. Or maybe it's the chilly jungle breezes in your tent.

Or maybe it's because you are turning to stone. You'll be famous when they find your stony body in the morning.

You'll be a regular ROCK STAR!

THE END

You reach out and shake Unger's hand. They're strange old women, but they seem to be friendly. Besides, you need all the help you can get!

"Can you help us find the Fireheart fruit?" you ask. "We read in a pamphlet that the Fireheart fruit is an antidote to the Muglani magic."

"Aha!" Unger shouts. "You read our pamphlet! We published that booklet to warn people about the Muglani!"

She looks very pleased that you read their booklet.

"You see, my sister was a victim of their magic. They shrank her head! I have it right in my bag to remind me to be on the lookout for them!"

"So that's why she has the head!" you murmur to Ben.

"Now, let's go!" Unger hollers. "We will take you to the Fireheart fruit right now! Then you will be a kid again!"

Excellent!

Turn to PAGE 62 to follow the Warrior Women.

"Well, to tell you the truth," you say hesitantly, "yes, I did."

As you see the king's face turn from gold to red, you start apologizing fast.

"You didn't say we couldn't go in there!" you stammer. "I didn't even know what the room was. I ended up in there by mistake. I'm sorry." You and Zoe start backing away from the king. You step down the first few steps of the pyramid.

"Seize them!" the king commands in a booming voice.

"That's not fair!" you shout. Now what are you going to do?

The cave creatures swarm forwards. They grab your arms and legs. Their hard rocky hands hurt your skin. It feels as if they're going to rip you apart!

Struggle to PAGE 97!

124

The footsteps are coming closer and closer. Quickly you duck under the table. The shrunken heads hanging down form a curtain. You pray you can't be seen. You watch from under the table as three pairs of legs enter the clearing. All three are wearing khaki trousers and army boots.

"What an odd little clearing!" says a British-sounding woman's voice. You see a woman bend down and touch the earth. She is wearing a full set of khaki fatigues and carrying a long hunting rifle.

She's a hunter! A jolt of fear blasts down your spine. What if she sees you? She might think you're an animal and shoot you!

"Some kids were here," she declares, patting the ground.

"Why, that's absurd!" another British-sounding voice answers. "Why would children be in the heart of the jungle?"

"James!" the woman declares sharply. She kneels on the ground. "I am Gwen Shripp, the world-famous hunter! I know the footprint of a trainer when I see one! I knew I should never have brought you on this expedition!"

"You're right, Gwen dear," James apologizes.

That's when Gwen, the world-famous hunter, turns and sees you hiding under the table. She quickly raises her gun!

DUCK out of the way on PAGE 115!

The icy water fills your eyes, ears and mouth. You gulp for air only to swallow water, cough and sputter. You thrash your arms but it feels as if you're still sinking! In your panic, you let go of your stick!

Your lungs begin to ache. You open your eyes and try to see what it is that has pulled you under.

It's no good. All you can see is the blurry blue of water. Water . . . water . . . everywhere . . .

With one last burst of strength you shake off the thing that has you by the foot. Gasping for air, you reach the surface. You look back in terror and see . . .

ZOE! She's red-faced and giggling.

"Zoe!" you shout. "You know I can't swim!"

"Sorry." She laughs, treading water. "You looked so scared staring into the cave like that! I just couldn't resist giving you a little dunk!"

"I'm not scared!" you protest. "I was just wondering if we'll be able to find a way out. It's so dark in there."

"Just wondering, huh?" Zoe teases. "Want *me* to go first?"

If you want Zoe to lead, then follow to PAGE 52.

If you want to go first, proceed to PAGE 83.

126

You are faced with the skeleton of a tiger.

This pit must be an old tiger trap! you think. Your knees feel as if they might give way.

The bones of the tiger are frail and decaying, but they glow with a ghostly iridescence. The tiger's tail whips from side to side, clattering like a rattlesnake. It opens its giant jaws to roar at you, but no sound rushes out. The tiger has no voice. All you hear is the tiger's tail rattling in the wind. That and the frantic beating of your heart.

The tiger steps towards you. One paw looks even more crushed than the rest of them. That must be the one you stepped on.

It rips through the air with its claws.

You step backwards . . .

CRUNCH!

RATTLE!

Looks like you've awakened the bones of another tiger. Hope you've got guts. It's two against one.

Quick! Flip to PAGE 25.

You duck to the right. The ant takes the tunnel to the left. It wasn't chasing you at all! It was only doing what ants do—moving things round!

Whew!

You glance round at the new branch of the tunnel you've chosen. The walls glitter! There are fat gems stuck in the stone!

Wow! You've never seen such beautiful gems before! The further you go down the tunnel, the more gems there are! You continue down the passageway into a cave.

Your mouth hangs open in wonder as you behold the beautiful cave. Huge stalactites hang down from the ceiling. They drip with jewels. Everywhere you look, light bounces off the gleaming facets of precious gems. The walls are crusted with rubies, emeralds, sapphires and diamonds.

You step round the stalagmites that protrude from the floor. Loose jewels are scattered by your feet.

There must be gold in here somewhere!

Search for gold on PAGE 45.

128

"I'll set the timepiece right here," you say to Zoe. You withdraw the miniature timepiece from your shirt pocket and set it carefully on the flat rock.

"I'm ready. Let's get out of here!"

There's a loud "CLICK" from the rock where you set the timepiece. The ledge slides into the wall! You have pressed a secret button of some sort!

Quickly you catch the hourglass as it slides off the disappearing rock shelf. Whew! That was close! It almost fell down the tunnel.

That's when you feel the grooves of the ladder you've been climbing start to flatten out. The ladder is becoming smooth—the whole tunnel is rounding out, turning into a big round chute! You can't hold on much longer!

Hurry to PAGE 73 to see what happens!

"I'll scare them away!" you whisper to Ben. "Watch this!"

You jump out from behind the big bush. Roaring like a monster from a horror film, you slash the air with your claws.

"Aaaaaargh!" Mrs Wheedle hollers at the top of her lungs. The rest of the kids scream in terror.

"Run!" Mrs Wheedle cries. And they scatter like flies.

All except for Bill Green, who just stands there with his mouth open. Finally, his brother grabs him by the arm and drags him into the brush.

"Nice going!" Ben says, taking off his glasses and wiping his eyes. He's laughing so hard, tears are streaming down his face.

"Did you see Mrs Wheedle's expression?" you ask with a chuckle.

Ben does a little imitation of Mrs Wheedle screaming. He dances round in a circle, flailing his arms. Suddenly he stops. An expression of true terror comes over his face. He points right at you.

"Mmmmu ... mmmu ... mmmu..." Ben stammers in fear.

"What's wrong?" you ask. "Are you okay?"

"Mmmmuglani!" Ben exclaims. "Behind you!"

Race to PAGE 111.

130

"Sorry, fish-guy!" you shout over your shoulder. "We've got to get back to the king!"

You splash through the pool and into the main tunnel.

"I can't believe we did it!" Zoe exclaims.

"I know!" you reply. "I'll almost be glad to see Mrs Wheedle!"

The two of you race into the throne chamber. The king of the cave people is pacing on the top of the pyramid. Only a few grains of sand are left in his tremendous timepiece.

"We have your gold!" you call to him.

All the cave creatures gather round as you and Zoe climb the steps to the top of the pyramid.

You kneel down in front of the king and pull Zoe down, too. Both of you present him with the gold you found.

"I see you have brought me the gold I requested," he states with his booming voice. You can see your reflection in his bulging eyes. His moss-covered face is serious and stern.

"I have just one question for you before I release you."

Oh, no! What more could he possibly want?

Flip to PAGE 70 to find out.

"Quick, Zoe, follow me!" you shout. You spin round and duck to the left, speeding past the cave people. No way are you going to stick around to introduce yourself to a gang of underground mutants!

You hear them grunt in surprise as you run by them. Zoe is right behind you.

You see a small tunnel off to the side in the great chamber. The tunnel is brightly lit. A good sign!

You barrel through the tunnel.

"Run!" Zoe yells, panting. "They're right behind us!"

It's true, you can hear them grunting to each other as they chase you.

Ahead of you the tunnel grows brighter and brighter. It's almost as bright as daylight. Maybe the tunnel leads to the outside!

Zoe shouts, "A door!" and points off to the right.

A small blue door is cut right into the side of the tunnel. Maybe the door leads outside!

You can try the door or you can just go straight. Either way, you'd better move fast. The cave creatures are gaining on you!

Do you stick to the tunnel? Keep going to PAGE 134.

Or do you try the blue door? Flip back to PAGE 40.

132

"Aargh!" you cry as you run away from the ant.

You hear its scuttling legs scratching the dirt behind you.

The huge ant chases you further and further into the maze. Over your shoulder you see its huge bug eyes and sharp pincers. That rock in its pincers must weigh a tonne.

If it can carry a boulder that big, it could probably snap your whole body in two with no problem at all.

Ahead of you the tunnel branches in two . . .

If you're wearing the colour blue, go to the left and to PAGE 93.

If you're not wearing blue, take the tunnel to the right and go to PAGE 127.

The dragon has you pinned to the ground! It snaps at your face with its razor-sharp teeth.

You get a crazy idea. You snap right back at the dragon. After all, you're a monster, too! You growl and gnash your own sharp teeth.

"Get off me!" you shout. You push the dragon off you and scamper to your feet.

Then something happens. Something unexpected. You take in a big puff of air and feel the back of your neck rising up.

It's not really your neck, but a flap of skin on your neck. It rises up and out like a hood behind your head!

It feels huge! And out of the corner of your eye, you can see that it's covered with bright and colourful markings. It makes you look bigger and scarier than you really are!

The dragon takes one look at you now and stops hissing. It starts to whimper instead. It cowers at your feet.

You let out a terrifying howl. The dragon slinks back to the tree with its head down.

Slink over to PAGE 66 yourself.

134

"Let's stick to this tunnel!" you yell to Zoe as you race from the cave people chasing you.

The light in the tunnel is so bright that you're sure you and Zoe are about to reach an exit. In another minute, you'll be back in the jungle. Then you can go and find Mrs Wheedle and the rest of the kids.

You glance behind you. The cave people on your trail are closing in!

You reach a ledge. The exit must be just beyond it. Kicking and pulling, you manage to hoist yourself up to the next level. Zoe does the same. A blast of hot air greets you.

Spread before you both is a pool of molten lava!

Quick! Turn to PAGE 102.

The king of the cave people peers down at you. All the features on his face are covered by soft golden fuzz. The thick horns stick out from the sides of his enormous round puff-ball head.

He's so tall that you're getting a cramp in your neck from looking up at him!

"We live in this mountain. It is our home. You have trespassed here," he says as he lowers himself majestically to his throne.

Zoe interrupts him. "Excuse me, Mr King, sir, I mean Your Highness, I mean, whatever your name is." Her face is turning red.

"Yes, what is it, human?" he asks impatiently.

"We're very sorry to have burst into your home like this. We really shouldn't be here," Zoe says, brushing her brown fringe out of her eyes as she always does when she's nervous. "If you'd kindly show us how to get back out, we'd gladly leave . . ."

"Ha-ha, very funny!" bellows the king. All the cave creatures start snorting and chuckling.

"Silence!" the king bellows, cutting his subjects off. He leans forward and grabs Zoe by the arm!

Find out what happens next on PAGE 116.

You look down at your hands. What used to be soft, pink skin is now rubbery grey flesh. Thin, transparent webbing connects each of your fingers. And each finger ends in a sharp claw!

How could this have happened? You *have* turned into a monster!

You reach up to feel your face. It's different from how it used to be. Instead of a nose, you feel two little airholes.

And your eyes have grown! They're huge! You blink and two clear flaps of skin skim over the surface of your gigantic eyes. A spiky ridge juts out from the top of your head, like a scaly mohawk!

Before you can even ponder what to do next, you hear the sound of someone walking through the jungle.

You don't think it's Zoe, either. She took off in the other direction. Who could it be?

Maybe it's someone who could help. SOME-BODY put that basket of fruit there and hung those shrunken heads. Maybe they would know how to get you back to normal again!

Then again, looking like you do, maybe you should hide.

They're coming closer. You can hear them humming. Quick! Make up your mind!

To get help from the person who is coming, turn to PAGE 7.

To hide, turn to PAGE 124.

Give Yourself Goosebumps

A scary new series from R.L. Stine – where *you* decide what happens!

Choose from over 20 scary endings!

m
Sink!

Goosebumps

R.L.Stine

Reader beware, you're in for a scare!

These terrifying tales will send shivers up your spine:

Goosebumps

Reader beware – here's THREE TIMES the scare!

Look out for these bumper GOOSEBUMPS editions. With three spine-tingling
stories by R.L. Stine in each book, get ready for three times the thrill …
three times the scare … three times the GOOSEBUMPS!

COLLECTION 1
Welcome to Dead House
Say Cheese and Die
Stay Out of the Basement

COLLECTION 2
The Curse of the Mummy's Tomb
Let's Get Invisible!
Night of the Living Dummy

COLLECTION 3
The Girl Who Cried Monster
Welcome to Camp Nightmare
The Ghost Next Door

COLLECTION 4
The Haunted Mask
Piano Lessons Can Be Murder
Be Careful What You Wish For

COLLECTION 5
The Werewolf of Fever Swamp
You Can't Scare Me!
One Day at HorrorLand

COLLECTION 6
Why I'm Afraid of Bees
Deep Trouble
Go Eat Worms

COLLECTION 7
Return of the Mummy
The Scarecrow Walks at Midnight
Attack of the Mutant

COLLECTION 8
My Hairiest Adventure
A Night in Terror Tower
The Cuckoo Clock of Doom

COLLECTION 9
Ghost Beach
Phantom of the Auditorium
It Came From Beneath the